ROGUE QUEEN

L. Sprague de Camp

A SIGNET BOOK from
NEW AMERICAN LIBRARY
TIMES MIRROR

SIGNET TRADEMARK REG. U.S. PAT. OFF. AND FOREIGN COUNTRIES
REGISTERED TRADEMARK—MARCA REGISTRADA
HECHO EN CHICAGO, U.S.A.

SIGNET, SIGNET CLASSICS, SIGNETTE, MENTOR AND PLUME BOOKS
are published by The New American Library, Inc.,
1301 Avenue of the Americas, New York, New York 10019

FIRST PRINTING, NOVEMBER, 1972

PRINTED IN THE UNITED STATES OF AMERICA

CAN WORKERS FIND
LIBERATION IN A LITTLE
GOLD BOX?

Iroedh looked up to see Barbe Dulac bearing down upon her. The female man held a small gold-colored box in her extended hand.

"Here you are, Iroedh dear."

"What's that?" said Vardh. "What does it do?"

"We Terran females use it to give ourselves the beauty," said Barbe.

"*How*?" inquired Avpandh.

Barbe opened the little box. "First here is a—how would you say mirror?"

The Avtini crowded around to look at their reflections in astonishment. It was like looking through a tiny window into another world.

"Now there is this. It is called a powder puff. Among us a shiny nose is considered ugly. Hold still, Iroedh . . ."

Barbe stood back from her handiwork. The three juniors looked at Iroedh and whooped with mirth.

"What's it supposed to do, to color our faces like this? Do you prepare for some ceremonial in this manner?"

"You might say so," said Barbe. "This is how one catches a male."

Other SIGNET Science Fiction You'll Enjoy

To
WILLY LEY

CONTENTS

AUTHOR'S NOTE: While the reader may pronounce the Ormazdian words in this story as he pleases, I offer the following suggestions: *i, e, a, o,* and *u* as in "police," "let," "calm," "more," and "rule," respectively; *y* when followed by a vowel as in "yet," when followed by *r* as in "myrtle," and otherwise as in "cyst." Vowels (other than *y*) have the same values in combination as singly; hence, *Gliid* is "glee-eed"; *Yaedh* "yah-edh." *Dh* represents the *th* in "the"; *lh* the voiceless *l* (Welsh *ll*); *rh* the voiceless *r* (Welsh *rh*); *kh* the velar fricative (German *ch*). As the last three sounds do not occur in English, they may be rendered as ordinary *l*, *r*, and *k*. *Viagens* (a Portuguese word) rhymes approximately with "Leah paints," with the *g* as in "beige." A glossary of Ormazdian words and names is appended to the book, but is not necessary to the understanding of the story. The quotation by Bloch in Chapter IX is from "The Oracles" from *Last Poems* by A. E. Housman. Copyright, 1922, 1950. Used by permission of Henry Holt and Company, Inc.

I. The Community

The messenger rose from her chariot seat and sharply cracked her whip. The ueg, its big hands gripping the shafts, craned its long neck around, grunted its indignation, and slightly speeded up the slap-slap of its big flat feet. Many-jointed creeping things scuttled across the wet sand of the beach and slipped with small splashes into the Scarlet Sea.

As soon as the rhythm of the ueg's two feet showed signs of slowing, Rhodh of Elham cracked her whip again. This ueg was an old bluffer, adept at appealing to its driver's sympathy. But with the hills behind them and only a half-hour's drive ahead, Rhodh (who was not given to squandering sentiment on dumb beasts anyway) had no sympathy to spare. For the news she bore was more important to the Community than the life of an ueg, or even of a worker like herself.

The chariot lurched and canted as the ueg cut in from the beach where the road took up again to cross the base of Khinad Point. Rhodh hardly glanced at the ruined towers of Khinam thrusting jaggedly up from the jagged rocks, though one of her fellow workers, Iroedh, had tried to interest her in the ancient artifacts to be found in the ruins. Such interest was all very well for drones, who had nothing better to do with their time between assignations than to make silly rhythmic noises, or even for Iroedh, who was a queer creature anyway.

But she, Rhodh, could never feel any fascination for the pastimes of her remote ancestors. No creatures with the bestial customs of her forebears, like those described in the *Lay of Idhios,* could produce anything worth the interest of a dutiful worker. Besides, her destiny lay higher than the collection of useless knowledge. Someday she'd sit on the Council and do something about round dances and other forms of time wastage. General Rhodh? Foreign Officer Rhodh? With her efficiency rating and moral superiority, there was nothing she could not do.

Rhodh cracked her whip again, this time against the ueg's leathery hide. The animal squawked and leaned forward in a run. This news must go to the highest officer at Elham; if the Council could not grasp the situation, then to the queen herself.

The sun was low in the hazy sky when Rhodh drew up at the outer wall of the Community. The guards, knowing Rhodh, let her through without formal identification. She drove on toward the cluster of interconnected domes that rose from the middle of the intramural park.

In front of the entrance she called *"Branio!"* to the ueg, hitched the beast, and walked stiffly up to the portal. Two workers stood guard on either side of the door, their freshly polished brazen cuirasses, studded kilts, greaves, and crested helmets blazing in the low sun. Their spears stood straight and their faces showed nothing but corpse-like calm.

Rhodh knew them. The one on the left was young Tydh, a sound regulation-minded worker; the other was the woolly-minded antiquarian Iroedh.

A few minutes before, these guards had been standing at ease while Tydh chattered and Iroedh ate a ripe vremoel and half listened, half daydreamed.

". . . and you'd think any fool would know better than to change queens with the war cry of the Arsuuni practically ringing in our ears. I know Intar's rate of laying is down, but so what? It's high enough for the purposes of the Community, but when the Council get an idea in their heads . . ."

Between bites Iroedh said: "We don't know that queens will be changed."

"Intar cannot refuse the challenge . . . Or do you think she will kill Princess Estir? Not likely; she's fat and wheezy, while Estir moves like a noag on the hunt and handles a spear like a soldier of Tvaarm. Of course there are those who say Intar's lucky. But for the conflict with the Arsuuni we need, not a lively young queen who can leap her own height and best an old one in the Royal Duel, but an old and crafty one who——"

Iroedh sighted Rhodh, finished her vremoel in one big bite, threw the pit into the shrubbery, and said: "Attention! A chariot's coming."

Tydh snapped upright but continued to talk. "That's Rhodh, who went to Thidhem on that project to plant a colony in Gliid. She's always rushing about on some mis-

12

sion or other; they say she'll make the Council yet. She was to get a quit-claim from Queen Maiur on the valley——"

"Belay the talk."

"But she's one of our own——"

"I said belay it."

As junior, Tydh perforce shut up while the chariot drew near and stopped. Iroedh watched Rhodh stamp up the steps in an umbrella hat, laced boots, and a traveling cloak of long-stapel suroel which because of the warmth was thrown back over both shoulders. Her only other item of wear was a sheath knife hanging from a light baldric. Her spear she had left in its boot in the chariot.

Iroedh watched her approach with mixed feelings. Once she had liked Rhodh, thinking she shared her own enthusiasm for the lost arts of antiquity. However, they had both been very young at the time, and later Rhodh's interest in Iroedh's hobbies had faded into the grim devotion to duty of the ideal Avtiny worker. For a while Iroedh had almost hated Rhodh in her disappointment, but then this feeling too had subsided into a vague regret for the loss of early promise.

Rhodh exclaimed in a voice high with tension: "Sisters, who is the highest officer of the Council at Elham now? I must see her at once!"

"Great Eunmar!" said Tydh. "What on Niond is the matter, Rhodh? Has another Community declared war upon us?"

"Never mind. Quick, who is she?"

"I'll check the list," said Iroedh. "The general is of course with the scouting force on the frontier of Tvaarm. The commissary officer has gone to Thidhem for the eight-day. The upbringing officer is sick. The foreign officer is with the general; the royal officer's at the queen's laying . . . By Gwyyr, not one officer of the Council is available!"

"That is impossible! The law requires at least one to be on duty at all times."

"The upbringing officer was supposed to be, but was taken with cramps. Meanwhile——"

"Then I must see the queen!"

"What?" cried Iroedh and Tydh together.

"Queen Intar of Elham, herself, at once!"

"Are you mad?" said Iroedh. "She's laying!"

"That cannot be helped. This news is more important than one egg more or less."

"Impossible, unless Queen Omvyr's soldiers have already attacked."

"This is even more momentous than that. At least we know all about the Arsuuni."

Tydh looked at Iroedh, who as senior would have the final say. "We dare not, Iroedh. The regulations are explicit. We should be punished."

Iroedh said: "Tell us your story, Rhodh, and I will judge."

Rhodh fanned herself with her wide-brimmed hat. "Stupid, stupid . . . But I suppose I must. Hmp. When the representative of Queen Maiur of Thidhem and I went to Gliid to rough out the bounds of the proposed colony, we arrived just as a—what would you call it?—an airship or sky ship alighted, bringing beings from the stars who call themselves *men*."

Iroedh and Tydh exchanged glances of puzzlement shading into consternation. The latter said:

"Impossible, Rhodh dear! It's been proved that the stars must be too hot to support life. Or is this a new version of one of those old legends Iroedh collects, about the gods' coming to earth?"

"I assure you," snapped Rhodh, "that I saw the creatures myself and talked to them. And nobody has ever accused me of lying. It seems that many stars are circled by worlds like ours, and many of these worlds support life. There is even a sort of interstellar government called the Interplanetary Council. These men are among the most advanced of the civilized species on these other worlds (or at least advanced in the natural sciences) and have sent their sky ship to discover us, as we might send a galley to look over an island in the remote regions of the Scarlet Sea."

As Rhodh paused for breath, Tydh said: "It's just as the Oracle of Ledhwid said:

"When the stars fall down and the waters rise
Then flowers of bronze shall grow on the dome;
And a drone shall be deemed uncommonly wise
When he seeks a new home."

Rhodh said: "I suppose you mean that when the sky ship comes all our drones will turn rogue. We'll see to *that!*"

"But what do these men look like? Are they many-legged like a dhwyg or all jelly like a huusg?"

"They are really quite human-looking, with certain differences."

"Such as?" said Tydh.

14

"Oh, they're a little shorter than we are, with skins of yellow and brown instead of red like ours; they have five digits on each hand and foot instead of four; their ears are large and wrinkled around the edge; their eyes have round pupils instead of slit pupils like ours; they have hair all over the tops of their heads instead of a single strip running from the scalp down the back as with us; and—well, that gives you an idea. What is more important is that they have no caste of workers!"

Iroedh spoke: "Then who built and manned this sky ship?"

"Their drones and queens. The ship's company consists mainly of drones, with two or three queens. When I asked where their workers were it took them a while to understand the question, and then the one who learned our language assured me they had none—all were functional males and females."

"What!" cried Iroedh.

"And you call them civilized?" said Tydh. "When they reproduce like animals?"

"I do not care to argue the point," said Rhodh. "I am trying to convince you that this arrival has enormous possibilities for good or evil to the Community, and it therefore behooves you to take me to the queen at once!"

Tydh said: "If you'll wait an hour, the queen will have laid and the royal officer will have certified the egg and placed it in the incubator——"

"No," said Iroedh, "I agree that the matter requires immediate attention. We will go to the queen——"

"But the regulations!" wailed Tydh. "We shall be punished——"

"I'll take responsibility," said Iroedh. "You stay here, Tydh."

Iroedh led the way through the corridors to the central dome. Outside the anteroom to the queen's chambers stood extra guards, for Princess Estir was practically of age and there must be no risk of a chance encounter before the formal fight for succession. In the anteroom sat a massive drone with a cheerful air. As Iroedh clanked across he said:

"Hello, beautiful!"

"Hail, Antis," said Iroedh. "You're on tonight?"

Antis grinned. "Right. She'd have me out of turn if she dared. And tomorrow, if I can—you know. How about it?"

"I have to work. Scrubbing."

"Sad; all work and no play will make Iroedh a dull girl, don't you think? Let me know when you get a day off."

Iroedh became aware that Rhodh was staring sternly at her. Just then the inner door opened and Iroedh told the worker who opened it:

"Guard Iroedh to see the queen, with Messenger Rhodh."

"She's laying this very minute! I cannot——"

"This is an emergency. The minute the egg is laid, inform me. I take responsibility."

The worker ducked back into the inner chambers and presently returned, saying: "It's been laid, and she'll see you. But she says your news had better be important."

Queen Intar's lounge chair overflowed with her sagging bulk. A worker operated on the queen's huge mammae with a breast pump. The egg lay in the sandbox, where the royal officer was marking code symbols upon it in crayon.

"Well?" snapped the queen. "Don't tell me you broke in upon my laying period just to inform me that old Maiur won't give up her nonexistent claims on Gliid! I've had workers whipped for less."

Iroedh said: "Many eggs, Queen. I take responsibility for this interruption. Pray let Rhodh speak."

Rhodh repeated her story with further details. Queen Intar leaned forward when she described the men's sexual organization, and asked:

"Could these self-styled functional males be mere male neuters, a caste of male workers corresponding to our neuter females?"

"No; at least they said such was not the case. We could not very well demand proof."

"Then does this discrepancy in numbers mean that their males much outnumber the females?"

"Again, no. In numbers they are about equal, but as the female is smaller and viviparous they seldom go in for anything so strenuous as exploration."

"A fine lot of females! Are they mammals like us, or do they feed their young on this and that?"

"They are mammals; the functional females had fully developed glands—though not so fine as yours, Queen."

Trust Rhodh, Iroedh thought, always to work in some little bootlicking compliment to her superiors. The queen asked:

"How are they fertilized?"

"I was not able to examine their organs, but——"

"I don't mean that; I mean what social code governs

16

the act? Do they go about it catch-as-catch-can, like the beasts?"

"On the contrary, they are governed by an elaborate code. During their long journey from their star, not one of all those males——"

"What star *is* that?"

"We cannot see it from here, but they pointed to the constellation Huusg. They call it Sol or Sun and their planet Terra or Yrth, depending upon the language."

"What are their intentions?" asked the queen.

"They say they wish merely to study our planet and to try to trace part of an earlier expedition which disappeared on Niond. At least they say it did."

"I've never heard of such a thing. Do you believe their peaceful protestations?"

Rhodh shrugged. "One cannot, without proof, believe the statements of beings not merely from another Community or of another race, but of another world. They may be truthful and harmless; Ledhwid only knows. Personally I am always suspicious of people who profess to be motivated by a passion for knowledge for its own sake, regardless of its utility."

She shot a sharp look at Iroedh as she said this. Queen Intar persisted in her questions:

"What did they think of us?"

"At first they seemed a little afraid of us, as indeed we were of them. After they learned we had no weapons but spears they became friendly enough, and appeared quite as amused by our account of our ways and achievements as we were astonished by them. This interpreter, called *Blos* or *Blok*, told me our caste system reminded him of a small flying creature called a *bii*, domesticated on his home world for its sweet secretions."

"I trust you didn't give them information that would be useful to an enemy!"

"No, no, I was careful. . . ."

At length the queen said: "I can certainly see those possibilities for good and evil. The omens have been hinting at some portentous development. If we could somehow use them against the Arsuuni . . . If, for instance, we could capture one and hold him as a hostage to compel the others——"

"Queen, I have tried to make clear that their powers are so far beyond ours that any violence would be sheer madness."

"Poof! What powers?"

"Could we build a ship like that?"

17

"N-no, but what of it? How can they harm anybody with their magical ship, save by dropping it on them? And if it's anything like a normal watership it would break like an egg if they tried it."

"They have other powers. I have seen one stand up to a charging vakhnag and point a little hollow metal rod at it, and *bang!* the beast fell dead with a hole through it you could put your head into."

"Did they tell you how this device worked?"

"No. When I asked, they became evasive."

"Clever rascals, it seems. What other devils' tricks have they to hand?"

"That is hard to say. I heard they had a device that tells whether a person is lying. There was so much new about them I couldn't absorb it all at once. I will make notes as I remember and write a report for the Council."

"Good." Intar turned. "My good Iroedh, you did well to bring Rhodh in without waiting to untangle the threads of protocol. Resume your watch, and, as I shall probably have further orders for you, don't leave Elham. By the way, on your way out tell that drone I shan't want him. I have other matters on my mind."

As Iroedh passed through the anteroom on her way out, she saw Antis pacing the floor and gave him the message.

"My luck!" Antis scowled, then brightened. "In that case, why shouldn't we take our supper over to the ruins? Ythidh guards the dronery tonight, and if I can neither elude nor bribe her my name's not Antis of Elham."

"Fine," said Iroedh. "But Antis dear, let me warn you again not to drop hints of our unsupervised amusements in front of others."

"I don't."

"You did before Rhodh just now."

"That stupid creature?"

"She's not so stupid she didn't understand what you were talking about. If she complains to the Council it could be unpleasant. She would, too."

"What do they think I'm going to do to you? What *can* I do besides eat supper and help you look for antiques?" He laughed heartily, showing a fine set of blue teeth. "Anybody'd think you were a functional female!"

Iroedh sniffed. "Sometimes I find your peculiar sense of humor positively revolting."

He waved a hand. "Forget it, beautiful. I shall see you at Khinam at sunset."

Iroedh had been back on watch for an hour and was beginning to look for her relief when Rhodh appeared, saying:

"Queen Intar has decided to send a party back to this sky ship to establish closer relations with the men. As senior member I shall head the party, the foreign officer being unavailable. The others will be Iinoedh, Avpandh, Vardh, and you."

Iroedh's face lit up. She was especially pleased that Vardh was coming, for Vardh had always looked up to Iroedh.

"What wonderful luck! Thank you, Rhodh dear!"

"Hmp! Don't thank me. I would never have chosen you, and I don't know why the queen did. This would never have happened if the Council had been functioning, but you know Queen Intar. The agricultural officer must have put in a word for you; we all know you're a pet of hers."

Iroedh listened first in astonishment and then in anger to this tirade. She flared:

"What have you got against me? I've traveled before, and my efficiency rating is well above the mean."

"It is not that, but these tales of your fraternizing with a drone, sneaking off on picnics with him and Ledhwid knows what else. He practically confirmed the rumor with his own words today."

"And what business is that of yours?"

"None, but you asked me why I didn't think you an ideal choice for this mission. Workers who associate with drones fall into dronish habits. They waste time, fool around, and take their pleasure when there is work to be done. They dance and plant flowers and that sort of nonsense. However, the next Cleanup will take care of that!"

Iroedh, who had reason to hate the word "Cleanup," made her face blank and replied coldly: "I suggest you defer judgment on my fitness for the mission until it's over. When do I report?"

"Tomorrow after brunch, in full campaign gear. Good night."

Iroedh watched Antis peck with his flint and pyrites until he had a small fire going, then slipped around to windward so as not to have to endure the smell of cooking meat. It was a measure of their affection that they were willing to eat together, the pleasure they got from each

19

other's company outweighing the disgust that the diet of each aroused in the other.

Out on the Scarlet Sea a great flying fish flapped and wheeled in circles, looking for smaller sea creatures to snap up, and silhouetted blackly against a blood-colored setting sun. Around them rose the ruins of Khinam, whose shattered spires and hypnotic mosaics the modern Avtini did not even try to imitate, let alone surpass. Near at hand rose the Memorial Pillar of Khinam, celebrating some forgotten hero or victory. Although the statue that crowned it had been eroded down to a mere pitted torso, the pillar itself, being of solid masonry, had survived better than most of the city's structures.

Antis, looking up from his fire making to watch the flying fish, remarked: "That's an omen of change."

"What is?"

"When a flying fish circles withershins."

"Oh, silly! You see omens in everything, and changes are always occurring."

Iroedh fell into a reverie as she absently munched her own meager meal of biscuits and vegetables while turning over her loot in the fading light.

"What," she said, "do you suppose this is? It's too frail for a weapon, and doesn't look like an ornament. A staff of office, perhaps?"

Antis looked up from the haunch of leipag he was roasting. "That's a telh, with which the ancients used to make music."

"How does it work?"

"You blow into that hole at the end and twiddle your fingers over the other holes. Remember that picture on the wall of the Throne Hall?"

Iroedh blew without result.

"Come to think," said Antis, "you don't blow into the hole, but across it—like that!" Iroedh's shift in position was rewarded by a wail from the flute. "Here, let me try it."

"Your hands are greasy!" said Iroedh.

"Very well, after I finish this. What's that book among the junk?"

Iroedh picked up an ancient volume from the litter. Its pages of vakhwil bark were cracked and crumbly, and the ink so faded that the text could not be read in the waning light. Above each line of writing ran a strip of fine parallel lines dotted with little black spots.

"A songbook!" cried Antis. "What luck!"

20

"I suppose those little black spots show what hole you close with your fingers?"

"Or more likely which you leave open. Try it."

Iroedh began blowing and fingering. Despite her inexpertness, a certain tune became recognizable.

"I think I know that one," said Antis. "When I was first admitted to the dronery there was an old drone named Baorthus who'd been let live through several Cleanups after his time because he was so skilled at his task. He used to hum a tune like that. I suppose I ought to have memorized it, but I was too occupied with my new function, and at the next Cleanup Baorthus got it. I'd forgotten all about it till now."

He wiped his hands on a weed and came to look over Iroedh's shoulder. "By Eunmar! With more light we could read the song and the notes at the same time, don't you think? Let me feed the fire."

He went out, leaving Iroedh to tweedle mournfully. There was a sound of breaking sticks and back he came with a bundle of fuel.

"Now," he said when the fire was blazing, "let's start at the beginning. You play, I sing." He scowled at the faint spidery letters. "A plague on this archaic spelling! Let's go:

> *"Love does not torment forever.*
> *Came it on me like a fire,*
> *Like the lava of Mount Wisgad,*
> *Or the blaze that sears a forest.*
> *When my love is not far distant,*
> *Do not think my sleep is easy;*
> *All the night I lie in torment,*
> *Preyed upon by love in secret . . ."*

Their performance was hampered by the fact that every line or two one or the other would get off the tune, and it finally broke up in a fit of mutual laughter.

When she could get her breath Iroedh asked: "What's this 'loved one' the fellow keeps talking about?"

"A friend, I suppose; a fellow member of the Community."

"I can't imagine losing sleep over a fellow worker; or even over you, my best friend."

Antis shrugged. "Ask the Oracle of Ledhwid. The ancients had some funny ideas. Maybe their lack of dietary control had something to do with it."

Iroedh mused: "The only time I ever saw an Avtin so

21

stirred was when that foreigner, Ithodh of Yeym, learned that her Community had been annihilated by the Arsuuni. She killed herself, even though the Council offered to admit her to Elham as a member."

"Well, no doubt we should be upset if we heard Elham had been wiped out. It may be yet, you know."

"Let's not think of anything so horrible before we must!"

"All right, my dear. Let me borrow the telh and the book, will you?"

"Certainly, but why?" said Iroedh.

"I thought I should have fun with my fellow drones. If you hear strange sounds from the dronery, it'll be Kutanas and I teaching them the ancient art of singing."

"I hope it won't cause the trouble the *Lay of Idhios* did!"

"And who taught me the *Idhios*?"

"I did, but only to keep it from dying out. I didn't expect a poetic orgy—"

"Just so; and neither shall these songs be let perish. After all, I shan't be around too much longer to cherish them."

"What do you mean?" she asked, knowing very well what he meant, but hoping against hope.

"One of these days there'll be a Cleanup, and I'm one of the oldest drones."

"Oh, Antis!" She seized his arm. "How dreadful! Has the queen been complaining?"

"Not so far as I know, and I've certainly been giving her upstanding service. But a Cleanup has been overdue for some time."

"But you're not really old! You're hardly older than I, and should be able to perform your duty for many years."

"I know, but that's not the Council's view. Maybe they're afraid we shall turn rogue if let live until we're old and crafty."

"You wouldn't ever, would you?"

"I hadn't thought about it. I suppose if you learned I was planning to escape and join the rogues you'd turn me in like a dutiful worker?"

"Of course. I mean I suppose so. It would be a dreadful decision to make. But don't plan anything so anti-Communitarian! Hold on as long as you can. You don't—I——"

Her voice choked off in a sob.

"Why, Iroedh!" said Antis, putting an arm around her.

"You sound like one of those ancients with their 'burning love.'"

Iroedh pulled herself together. "I'm foolish. And I'm no ancient, but a neuter worker and proud of it. Still, life would be so utterly empty without you."

"Thanks." He gave her a friendly squeeze.

"Nobody else in Elham shares my love for antiques. Sometimes I feel as a solitary rogue must feel, wandering the woods and looking in on the domes of the Communities he can never enter again."

Antis grinned in the gathering dark. "I can reassure you on one point, darling: If I should ever plan to go rogue, I won't confide in anybody who might spoil my plan."

She shivered. "Br-r-r. We should have brought clothing with us. Let's go back."

II. The Sky Ship

"Remember," said Rhodh, "we have two objectives: to use these men and their knowledge against Tvaarm, and to keep them from learning anything they might use against us."

Her ueg trotted beside that of Iroedh along the stretch where the road to Thidhem became one with the beach of the Scarlet Sea. The chariots of Iinoedh, Avpandh, and Vardh bumped along behind.

Rhodh continued: "So keep your eyes and ears open and your mouth, as far as possible, shut. There is so much new about these men that none of us can grasp it all at once. Flatter them, get them to brag, anything to loosen their tongues. But don't encourage them to visit us, tell them where Elham is, or reveal our political situation or methods of warfare. I am speaking particularly to you, Iroedh, because I know your weaknesses. They are interested not only in us but also in our history, and would like nothing better than to be guided to Khinam to look for relics. Then all they would have to do is to climb one of the towers to see the domes of Elham."

"I'll be careful," said Iroedh, bored almost to the

screaming point because Rhodh had been through all this before. She wanted Rhodh to leave her alone so that she could get back to her golden daydreams of ancient times.

"Your task will be to cultivate Blok, who speaks Avtinyk after a fashion and, like you, is interested in many different philosophies. If you apply yourself diligently to your task you will forget all about that drone you so imprudently befriended."

"Why should I?" said Iroedh in a louder voice than she intended. There went her good resolution not to let Rhodh bait her!

"Don't shout. You had better begin soon, because he will no longer be around on our return."

"You mean——"

Rhodh turned a cruel smile toward Iroedh. "Didn't you know? The Council collected a quorum this morning just before we left and fixed the date for the next Cleanup. It was decided to kill the three senior drones: Antis, Kutanas, and Dyos, to make room for the next crop, some time this eight-day. They were of course confined to balk escape."

Iroedh's rose-red skin paled a shade. Eunmar blast them! So that was why Antis hadn't said good-by. First she had thought he must be angry; then she wondered if he'd forgotten (which was unlike him); then she speculated as to whether he was trying to protect her by minimizing their attachment. When all the while . . .

"*Weu!*" she said in a choked voice. "You might have told me sooner."

"And have you throw an emotional scene or balk at your orders, and hold up our departure? I'm not so stupid. You will live to thank me yet."

"Why was such an early date chosen for the Cleanup?"

"Because of that prophecy Tydh cited, about a drone's seeking a new home. It was feared that if the drones heard of it they would desert in a mass. And it is not really an early date; one has been due for some time. Antis will certainly be no loss; there is no place in a well-run Community for his japes and scrapes."

Iroedh subsided, her mind in turmoil. She even thought of wheeling her chariot around and dashing back to Elham, but lifelong discipline and ingrained devotion to the Community stopped her. Besides, what would she accomplish except to get herself punished?

What to do? Though a mature worker, Iroedh had not yet settled into fatalistic acceptance of the tragedies of life. There must be something . . .

24

Why should Rhodh gloat? Iroedh could think of no reason for Rhodh to hate her. She had done nothing except be herself. That must be it; Rhodh, outwardly contemptuous of Iroedh's interest in the ancient arts, secretly envied her it. Or perhaps Rhodh was simply one with a passion for uniformity, to whom Iroedh's heterodoxy represented a social eyesore to be extirpated.

Iroedh's mind went back into its little revolving cage: How to save Antis? There must be something. No, nothing. But there must be, if she could only be clever enough to think of it. What, then? If I could only think of it. How do you know there is anything to think of? There simply must be. But that's wretched logic; things don't exist because you wish they did. . . .

She pondered the matter for hours while they drove past the place where the beasts had devoured the unfortunate Queen Rhuar, and over the Lhanwaed Hills where forgotten legends told of an egg the size of a royal dome waiting to hatch out—what, nobody knew. Iroedh had come to no conclusion when they reached the frontier of Thidhem.

Here they were stopped by a pair of guards whose armor bore the symbol of Queen Maiur. Rhodh identified herself to the senior of these guards, Gogledh.

"I know you, Rhodh," said Gogledh in the dialect of Thidhem. "I met you when you came here about the Gliid colony. Is this a surveying party, or what? When will the first colonists go out?"

Rhodh replied: "No, we are investigating the sky ship. What is Thidhem doing about it?"

"Nothing. Queen Maiur feels that contact with visitors having customs so different from ours might unsettle our social structure. She is even trying to stop all discussion of the event—which you know as well as I can't be done."

"Has your Council no say?"

"In theory, yes, but in practice Maiur usually gets her way. How about your colony?"

"No colony until the war with Tvaarm has been settled. If it comes we shall need every worker who can wield a spear."

Gogledh said: "You have a princess near her majority, whom you were going to send to Gliid, haven't you?"

"Yes; Estir. She matures in about another eight-day."

"And if you don't send her out with the new colony, there will have to be a Royal Duel, won't there?" Gogledh added eagerly. "And maybe there'll be passes for visitors from Thidhem?"

"I don't know; that will be up to the Council."

"Oh. Well, have the Arsuuni moved yet?"

"Not the last I heard. Our general's on the frontier watching."

"Poor Elham! I wish, just once, an Avtiny Community would overcome one of the Arsuuni."

Rhodh sighed. "We will do our best, but what can we accomplish against a caste of soldiers half again our size? We should need not only luck but also a great superiority in numbers, which we do not have."

"How many adult workers have you?"

"About four hundred and fifty. There would have been more but for last year's plague."

Gogledh said: "It's too bad there is no method by which our workers and yours could both fight the Arsuuni at once."

"Yes, isn't it? But that is the way of things. They are too shrewd to attack both our Communities at the same time."

On the afternoon of the third day, after Gogledh had left them, the five Elhamny workers entered the valley of Gliid.

Iinoedh cried: "Oh, look!"

Down near the center of the valley, dull-gleaming in the sunshine, rose a cylindrical object that could only be the sky ship, standing upon its base like the Memorial Pillar of Khinam, and tapering to a blunt point at the upper end.

Even Rhodh, normally a stranger to such emotions, seemed stirred. She said: "Let's hurry!" and cracked her whip.

The five vehicles filed down the winding road into the valley. Vardh said:

"I'm so excited; I've never been to Gliid! What's that strange-looking pinnacle springing out from the cliffs?"

She pointed. Iroedh explained:

"That's Survivors' Point."

"What does the name mean?"

"It refers to the last survivors among the bisexual Avtini, two thousand years ago."

"You mean when Queen Danoakor rationalized the diet of the race?"

"Yes," said Iroedh.

Iinoedh asked: "What became of the survivors?"

"They were besieged sixty-fours of days. One account says that when Danoakor's army reached the Point, the bisexuals were all dead of starvation; another asserts that they leaped off the cliff to their deaths."

"How dreadful!" said Vardh.

"Served them right," snapped Rhodh over her shoulder. "We should forget about those bestial savage days. If I had my way I would destroy every historical record. If it weren't for dronish sentimentalists like Iroedh, we should have done away with all that rubbish long ago."

The three younger workers subsided, as prudent juniors do when a quarrel impends among their seniors. Iroedh for her part said nothing because her mind was too full of reveries about the survivors and their tragic fate, of speculations about the impending meeting with the men, and the ever-present nagging worry over the doom of Antis.

As the sky ship loomed nearer, Iroedh was struck by the vast size of the thing. You could crowd a whole Community into it, assuming it was all hollow and not filled with the magical machinery of the men.

Things moved around the base of the sky ship. Evidently, Iroedh thought, those within had seen the column of chariots from afar. Rhodh, with Queen Intar's guidon whipping at the head of her spear, drove along the overgrown road to the open space where the thing had alighted. This space looked as though it had been cleared by the landing itself, for trees and shrubs were burned to ashes in a wide circle around the object.

One of the men stood where the burned circle touched the edge of the road. Iroedh looked it over as Rhodh, with a clang, jumped down from her chariot and the rest followed suit. Iinoedh gathered up the reins of the five uegs while the rest crowded forward.

The man was about Iroedh's height, quite Avtiny-looking despite its other-worldly origin. It was of slim build like a worker or princess, not burly like a drone or fat like a queen. It was covered with a substance that Iroedh at first thought to be a queer loose skin, but which closer scrutiny showed to be clothes, cut and stitched in various intricate ways to hug the body: boots not unlike those of the Avtini, but higher; a garment like a tunic with short sleeves; and another garment which Iroedh could only have called a leg tunic, or forked kilt, covering the creature from waist to calf where the legs of the garment disappeared into the boots. The whole was held together by an assortment of buttons and belts so complicated to Iroedh's eye that she wondered how the man had any time left after putting on and taking off these intricate vestments.

Though Rhodh had spoken of the men as having "hair all over the tops of their heads," this one had no hair on top at all, but a bare pink scalp with a fringe of brownish hair around the sides and back and another smaller fringe on the upper lip. Iroedh found the blue of its eyes startling, since most of the eyes she was familiar with were yellow.

In the crook of one arm it held an object something like a large version of the flute she had found in Khinam: a wooden stock or handle whence a dark metal rod or tube projected, the whole thing about as long as the man's arm, with mysterious knobs and projections. Then Iroedh remembered: This must be one of the men's magical weapons. She hoped the man would not be seized with an urge to point it at her and cause it to make a hole in her one could stick one's head into.

The man's cheeks drew back, exposing teeth of a surprising yellow-white. Rhodh, Iroedh thankfully remembered, had warned her not to be alarmed by this gesture. It meant, not that the man was going to bite, but that it was pleased; the act was in fact the Terran equivalent of a smile, which among the Avtini was of course made by rounding the mouth into an O.

The man spoke: "Hello, Rhodh! I did not expect you back so soon. Another worker was just here, from a place called Ledhwid. I see you have brought company."

It spoke Avtinyk slowly, with a thick accent and many mistakes. Iroedh was a little puzzled by the statement about "bringing company," which anybody could see for herself. Perhaps such a meaningless statement was a ceremonial gesture, of which the men employed many. Just as a worker meeting a queen said: "Many eggs!"

Rhodh said: "This is my next junior, Iroedh," and went on to introduce the rest.

The man said: "I am Bloch—Winston Bloch, and I am surely pleased to know you."

Vardh spoke: "Do you mean Winston *of* Blok? Is Blok your Community?"

"No; it is my—uh—one of my names."

"You mean you have more than one?"

"Yes. Three, in fact."

"Why?" asked Vardh.

"Too complicated to explain now."

"At least tell us the proper manner of addressing you."

"On Terra they call me Dr. Bloch. What can we do for you?"

28

"Iroedh will tell you," said Rhodh. "The rest of us will set up a camp nearby, if you have no objections."

"None at all," said Bloch with a wary air. "My dear Iroedh, would you care to—uh—step into our ship?"

"Thank you. I should like to see the whole ship," said Iroedh, not knowing quite how to handle the situation but plunging ahead anyway.

Bloch gave its head a shake. "I fear that is impossible. We are overhauling for the return trip, and you would get—uh—what do you call *grease?*—dirt all over your pretty pink skin. But come on; we will have a cup of coffee."

"*Kothi?*" said Iroedh, walking beside him toward the ship.

"Coffee, with a *ff*. You shall see."

"Has your ship a name?"

"Sure; do you see those letters? They spell *Paris*, the name of one of our—ah—Communities."

"Are you really a functional male?"

Bloch looked at her with a curious expression. "Of course!"

"And yet you *work?*"

"Certainly. Our males are not at all like your drones, who exist for one purpose only. Though I dare say there are those among us who would not find that such a bad deal." He tilted his head back and shouted in his own tongue: "Ahoy! Let down the hoist!"

Though she did not understand the words, Iroedh was taken with a desire to run away, for it had just occurred to her that these creatures might seize her for a hostage, or for a specimen to take apart. It would be just her luck. Yet Rhodh and her squad were over on the far side of the clearing. Having taken off their armor and the loose wrap-around tunics they wore under it to keep it from chafing, they were setting up their camp in apparent unconcern. And here came a thing like an oversized bucket dangling down on the end of a chain of gray metal. No doubt Iroedh was serving her Community by risking her life in the clutches of the men, but . . .

Bloch swung his legs over the side of the bucket, saying: "Hop in!"

Oh well, thought Iroedh, what did anything matter if Antis would be dead when she returned? She climbed in. The hoist rose.

Iroedh glanced over the side, then seized the edge of the car in a frenzy of panic. Her eyes bulged. She tried to speak but could only croak. Her stomach heaved so that

29

she thought she would lose her hours-old brunch. With a little moan she curled up on the floor of the vehicle, hands over eyes.

She had never before been dangled in mid-air without a tree trunk or other support in plain sight, and found the experience terrifying beyond all recollection. As the hoist rose, the hum of the hoisting machinery came louder and louder to her ears.

"Cheer up," said Bloch's voice; "the chain has never broken yet. Here we are."

Iroedh, feeling a little ashamed, forced herself to rise. Clutching the handrail with a deathly grip and refraining from looking down, she climbed after Bloch onto the platform against which the bucket now hung.

She went through the entrance, observing that the ship was built of the same gray metal as the hoist. She asked:

"What is the ship made of, Daktablak?"

"We call it *steel*—or rather *iron*. It is the common metal that is harder than copper and its—what would you call a mixture?"

"Alloys? We know no metal harder than cold-worked bronze. We have gold and silver, but they have only a few special uses."

She fell silent as they ducked through passageways into the little wardroom. It was crowded with other men, both male and female. Iroedh recognized the females by their smaller size and their breasts, despite the fact that, like the males, they were clothed.

She now realized that Bloch must be tall for his kind, for all the others were shorter than he. Their colors ranged from pale yellow-pink through various tans and bronzes to a brown that was almost black. Perhaps, she thought, different races were represented on the ship, though how they associated without trying to exterminate one another, as did the races on Niond, she did not understand.

Bloch introduced her, beginning with a dark brown man almost as tall as he but much fatter, wearing brass buttons on his tunic: "Captain Subbarau; Miss Dulac, my assistant; Mr. O'Mara, our photographer ..."

He went on through other names until they ceased to register in Iroedh's mind: "Norden, Markowicz, el-Jandala, Kang, Lobos, Cody ..." Most of them she could not have pronounced even if she could have remembered them.

At last they were all gone but Captain Subbarau, O'Mara, Miss Dulac, and Bloch. The photographer was shorter and thicker than Bloch (though not so stout as Subbarau) with wavy black hair and blunt features. Subbarau looked at him and said:

"O'Mara!"

The man gave the others what Iroedh interpreted as a sour look and went. Bloch and the Dulac female stared at his back, and Iroedh caught an impression of tension.

"Now," said Subbarau, "we shall have a spot of coffee and cake. I trust, my dear Iroedh, they won't poison you. They didn't hurt your friend Rhodh when she was here before. Take off your helmet if you like."

Bloch translated, and the conversation proceeded creepingly with much fumbling for words. Iroedh was glad to take off her helmet, as she was tired of bumping the crest against the overhead.

Bloch said: "Captain, when I asked them what we could do for them by way of making conversation, their leader said Iroedh would tell us."

Subbarau gave a thin version of the startling Terran smile. "I take it they want something. How different from the rest of the Galaxy! Say your say, Madame Iroedh."

Iroedh told of the war with the Arsuuni, feeling her way nervously. For all she knew, these strangers might be the sort who always sided with the stronger party.

"So," she concluded, pausing between phrases for Bloch to translate, "if you could destroy Tvaarm with your magical weapons, we should be everlastingly grateful and would promise to support your interests among the Communities on Niond."

The men exchanged glances. Iroedh, feeling that this was not going too well, faltered:

"We could pay you. We have large stores of cereal grains, and of the suroel fibers we make our cloaks from. We even have a fair supply of the gold and silver from which we make our queens' regalia and other ornaments."

Subbarau and Bloch conversed briefly and then the latter turned to Iroedh. Though she could not interpret his expression, he sounded sympathetic.

"It is not a matter of payment, Iroedh. If we could we would do it for nothing—that is, if conditions are as you describe them. But while we do not wish to injure your feelings, your grain and gold would be of no value to us unless we were marooned here by a failure of the ship. Our real reason for refusal is that our orders strictly forbid us to interfere in the local affairs of any planet, regardless of our sympathies."

"Even to help a peaceful Community defend itself against wrongful and unprovoked aggression?"

"Even that. Why are the Arsuuni attacking you?"

"It's their regular method of providing for their natural increase. Instead of building themselves new Communities, they seize ours and occupy them, and make slaves of such of our workers as survive the fighting."

"Well, you perceive how it is. Not that I doubt your story, but every combatant always has an adequate justification for his position. When we land on a strange planet, the first people we meet are likely to have hereditary enemies over the hill and to give us a dozen excellent reasons for helping them to exterminate these foes. If we yield to the temptation we are likely to discover that we have destroyed the side with the better cause, at least according to our way of thinking, or that we have antagonized half the inhabitants of the planet. The only sure method of avoiding such *gaffes* is a rigid rule against interference."

Iroedh cautiously sipped her coffee. It seemed like a bitter beverage to drink for pleasure, but if it hadn't poisoned Rhodh it probably would not kill her. She must keep trying to hook the space travelers into some kind of commitment. Not only was the life of the Community at stake, but also she had vague hopes of using diplomatic success as a lever to free Antis.

"Then," she said, "why not give us some of your magical weapons? A few—even one—might turn the scale."

Subbarau whistled.

"It need not be a permanent gift," said Iroedh, not knowing the meaning of the strange sound but suspecting it to be an unfavorable indication, "but a mere loan. You need not fear we should try to use it against you."

Bloch said: "You do not understand, my dear Iroedh. This is a ship of the *Viagens Interplanetarias*, the Terran space authority. Off Terra it is subject to the rules of the Interplanetary Council. One of this Council's regulations forbids introducing to—uh—backward planets inventions or technical knowledge these planets do not already possess."

"What do they mean by 'backward'?"

"Planets that have not attained a certain standard of development in science, law, ethics, and politics."

"What is the purpose of this rule?" asked Iroedh.

"That is a long story, but the gist of it is that they do not wish to arm some warlike race that might then irrupt out of its home planet and cause trouble elsewhere."

"Why doesn't our world qualify as civilized? We have an advanced culture, with writing, metalworking, large buildings, and a high degree of social organization. What more do you wish?"

"One of the first requirements is a single government for the entire planet. You do not have that, do you?"

"Great Gwyyr, no! Whoever heard of such a thing?"

"And you have not abolished the institution of war, have you?"

"Nobody has even thought of getting rid of it. It is part of the nature of things."

"There you are. Speaking of which, why does not your Community combine with some of its neighbors like Thidhem and smash the Arsuuni before they destroy you piecemeal?"

"Now it's you who don't understand, Daktablak. One Community could never combine with another, because the general of one would have to admit that the queen of another was equal or superior in authority to her own. And as the nominal supremacy of each queen in her own Community is the first principle of our society, such a course is out of the question."

"What do you mean by nominal supremacy?" asked Bloch.

"The actual governing is done by the Council, elected by the workers. The queen reigns but does not rule."

"Strict constitutional monarchy," said Bloch to Subbarau; then, to Iroedh: "I am sorry, my dear, but that is the best advice we can give you. If some irrational rule of your society prevents, so much the worse for your society. Now then, what is interesting around here? As a xenologist ———"

"As a what?" queried Iroedh.

"A xenologist; an expert on worlds other than my own. Anything is grist to my mill: geology, climate, plants, animals, people, science, history, art—practically anything you could mention. We have already secured a good collection of the plants and animals of this locale, however. Nearly all your land animals seem to be bipeds with no hair except occasional ornamental patches, like that crest on top of your head. Is that the case with the other continents?"

"As far as they are known to us, yes. Why shouldn't it be? Are things different on other worlds?"

"They certainly are. On our planet most animals walk on all fours and have hair all over, and on Vishnu most land life has six limbs."

"Why?" said Iroedh.

"Various reasons. For instance, the type of planetary motion and the distribution of land and water on our planet give it a more variable and extreme climate than yours, so the animals had to develop hair to keep warm during the cold seasons. But to get back: Are there any Communities hereabouts that we could see?"

"I don't think any Communities would admit you until they knew you better—unless you forced your way in, and I hope you won't do that."

"Then must we fly off to some other continent where the people are more approachable? We can give each continent only a limited time on a preliminary reconnaissance like this."

"The Avtini aren't unfriendly, but we can't take chances until we know more about you." When they looked at her silently she rushed on: "There are other things I'm sure will interest you. For instance, there are the ruins on Survivors' Point, in plain sight of this sky ship."

"Survivors' Point?" said Bloch.

Iroedh told them the story of the last bisexual Avtini, adding: "The remains of their fortress are still up there, if you can climb."

"How much of a climb is it? We can climb, but not vertically up the cliff face."

"You wouldn't have to. The old trail that leads up the side of the valley is still usable though somewhat overgrown."

"What is up there?" asked Bloch.

"You'll find many relics of former times. The fort was rebuilt fifty-odd years ago, when a band of rogue drones used it as a base."

"Not a bad idea," said Bloch. "Would you guide some of us up tomorrow?"

"Gladly. What time will be convenient?"

"A couple of hours after sunrise, let us say."

"That will be fine. Let's each of us bring her own food, as we might not find each other's fare palatable."

After Iroedh had left the *Paris,* Bloch asked Captain Subbarau: "How do you like our little redskin this time?"

"Better than the other one," replied Subbarau thoughtfully. "It gives one a curious sensation, like talking to an intelligent ant or bee in quasi-human form."

"They're not, really; it's just their familial organization. You mustn't press the parallel too far. They're intelligent, not instinctive like those fellows on Sirius Nine. And bees don't have democratically elected councils."

"True. If one filled her—— Should I refer to Iroedh as 'her' or 'it'?"

"I think of her as 'her.' After all, you call a girl baby 'her' even though she's no more sexually developed than Iroedh."

"Well, if you filled her out a little here"—Subbarau made motions with his cupped hands in front of his chest—"and put a wig of real hair on her head instead of that feathery Iroquois crest, she wouldn't make a bad-looking human female. If your taste runs to pink six-footers with cats' eyes. Are they as backward as they seem? They don't appear to have iron, let alone machinery."

"Funny about that. From all I can gather, they had a progressive culture up to two thousand of their years ago, when they adopted this sex-caste system. Since then they've not only stagnated, they've actually retrogressed."

"Perhaps they adopted a materialistic view, like the Earthly West, and it stultified their spiritual development?"

"Don't start that again, boss! Their sciences have stopped too. As for their religion, it's all gone except for petty superstitions and curses. They're great ones for omens and oracles, but the emotions that used to find a religious outlet are now devoted to their Communities."

"You mean hives," said Subbarau.

Rhodh told Iroedh: "Perhaps I was mistaken in sending you to deal with them. As far as I can see, all you accomplished was to shirk your share of the work of setting up the camp."

"I had nothing to do with their refusal," said Iroedh with heat. "I told you, they're bound by the rules of their own government."

"In any case, I had better deal with them tomorrow. What have you planned?"

Iroedh told of the projected expedition to Survivors' Point, adding: "I pray you let me guide them. If another takes my place tomorrow, they'll wonder if we've fallen out. Besides, I have much more in the way of common interests with Daktablak than you."

"I do not think——"

"Give me one more day," said Iroedh, forcing herself to adopt a wheedling tone. "Anyway, it's a two hours' climb, and I know the way. Have you ever been there?"

"I waste the Community's time visiting worthless ancient rubbish? Hmp! Go ahead, then, with your silly men. Truth to tell, I'm just as glad not to spend time on this trip that could be put to better use in ordering the camp so that it reflects credit on Elham."

That night Iroedh hardly slept at all.

III. Survivors' Point

Next morning as Iroedh walked toward the *Paris,* Bloch stood awaiting her. With him were the female man named Dulac and the male one called O'Mara, the latter with a rectangular leather case slung from one shoulder. Bloch again bore his mysterious weapon.

"Camera," said O'Mara in answer to Iroedh's question, which left her no wiser.

Bloch explained: "A magical picture-making machine. He comes on all these expeditions to make them."

"And what are those? Ornaments?" Iroedh pointed to a row of brass clips in Bloch's belt, each clip holding a number of little brass cylindrical things.

"They're for this." Bloch indicated the tube of dark metal, which Iroedh had learned was called a *gon* or *gyn.*

"What's that you're saying, Baldy?" said O'Mara. "Don't go blackguarding me to the young lady, now, just because I don't speak the heathen dialect of her."

Iroedh, not understanding this speech, led the party along the road by which the Avtini had entered the valley. O'Mara made a peculiar shrill noise with his mouth, like that which Subbarau had made the previous day.

"What's that?" asked Iroedh.

"We call it whistling," said Bloch, and tried to show her how. But though she puckered and blew, nothing came out but air.

She gave up and said: "Daktablak, you've asked many questions about our sex castes. Perhaps you'd tell me how your Terran sex system works?"

When Bloch had given her a brief account of Terran

36

monogamy, she said: "Does it make you men happier than we?"

"How should I know? One cannot measure happiness with a meter, and anyway I am not intimately enough acquainted with your people to judge. Among men, some esteem the system highly while others find it extremely distressing."

"How so?"

"Take Subbarau. He is unhappy because his female refused any longer to hibernate in a trance while he was away on his space trips, which take many years each, and left him for another male. And he comes from a country called India, where they take a serious view of such actions."

"Then you must age greatly during such a trip!"

"No, because of the Lorenz-Fitzgerald effect, which slows down time when you go almost as fast as light so that to those on the ship the trip seems to consume only a fraction of the time it actually does."

"I don't understand."

"Confidentially, neither do I, but it does operate that way. Of course this is hard on the mates of the ship people who are left home, so they usually take a medicine that puts them into a profound sleep, in which they do not age appreciably, while their partners are gone."

"How about you? Have you such a mate, and if so, is she on the ship or back on Terra?"

"I am single, unmated, and quite satisfied with my state."

"Like a rogue drone?"

"I suppose so, though I do not rob people as I understand they do."

"How about the Dylak?" asked Iroedh, glancing back to where Barbe Dulac plodded beside O'Mara, each looking frozenly forward. The longer legs of Iroedh and Bloch had enabled them to draw ahead of their companions.

"Oh, she is unhappy also."

"How?"

"She and O'—the man walking beside her—how would you say 'fell in love'?"

There followed several minutes of a search for synonyms, at the end of which Iroedh exclaimed: "I know what you mean! It's our word *oedhurh*, which now means devotion to one's Community, but which was used by the ancients in the sense of that violent emotion you describe. I've come across it in that sense in some of the old songs

37

and poems. But how can you 'fall into' a condition like that? One 'falls into' a hole in the ground . . ."

When Bloch had straightened her out on English figures of speech, she asked: "Are all men subject to this passion?"

"Some more than others. In the culture of my people, for instance, it plays a substantial part, whereas Subbarau's countrymen take a more detached view of it."

"But you said it made him unhappy."

"I think that was more hurt pride than love."

"And what happened to those two people behind us?"

"They got en—they entered into a contract to mate permanently, such as I told you about."

"Something like when a drone is initiated into adulthood and swears to serve his queen?"

"Yes. They got engaged, as we say, but then Barbe found her man was not what she had thought. He is what we call a roughneck——"

"A rough neck? You mean he has bumps on the skin of his neck, like the creeping thing called an umdhag?"

"A manner of speaking. He is a domineering fellow with a frightful temper, and she would not have fallen for him——"

"You mean she fell out of a window or something to please him? A strange custom——"

"Would not have fallen in love with him, I mean, if they had not been cooped up together so long on the ship. So she broke the engagement, and he has been in a rage ever since. He only insisted on coming along today to make things unpleasant for the rest of us."

"Because he's unhappy, then, he wants everybody else to be unhappy too?"

"That is about it."

"We sometimes have workers like that," said Iroedh, thinking of Rhodh.

"And he is frightfully jealous of me," continued Bloch, "because she works with me all the time, preparing my specimens and transcribing my notes."

"Why, are you in love with her?"

"I—uh—what?" Bloch looked at her with a startled expression, then said: "No, no, nothing of the sort," and cast a furtive glance at the two following. "But he thinks I am."

To Iroedh his protestations sounded too vehement to be altogether convincing. She asked:

"Could it be that you really are, Daktablak, but dislike

38

to admit it because you fear the wrath of that strong man?"

"Ridiculous, young lady. Let us talk of something else."

"If you wish, though I fear I shall never understand you mysterious men. And your kind of love can't be worth much if it makes everybody so unhappy. Here we turn off."

She led them along a trail that ran from the road across the floor of the valley. Bloch said:

"Iroedh, have you ever heard of another space ship's landing here, before the *Paris?*"

"No. We have ancient myths of gods coming down from the sky, but nobody believes them any more."

"This was only a few years ago, comparatively speaking. A mixed Osirian-Thothian expedition——"

"What sort of expedition?"

"One manned by people from the planets Osiris and Thoth, in the Procyonic system. Procyon is the second brightest star in the sky from here."

"You mean Ho-olhed?"

"Whatever you call it. The Osirians are something like your uegs, but with scales all over, while the Thothians are only about so high"—he held out a hand at waist level—"and are covered with hair. Their ship alighted on what I think is this same continent, judging from their descriptions and photographs. But after they had been here only a few days a party they had sent out to reconnoiter was attacked. When the only survivor got back to their ship——"

"Who attacked them?" asked Iroedh.

"Avtini, from the account; probably a band of those rogue drones you tell about. Anyway, the survivor told such a wild tale that the captain, an Osirian named Fafashen, got panicky and ordered them to take off for their own system at once. Osirians are really too impulsive and emotional for space exploration."

"I haven't heard of any such thing; but then it might have happened many sixty-fours of borbi from here, and such news wouldn't travel far because one Community normally neither knows nor cares what goes on in the territory of another. The few people like me who are interested in the race as a whole are looked upon as queer."

"I have heard that before too," said Bloch.

The trail now wound slantwise up the slope. Knowing what she faced, Iroedh had worn nothing but her boots and a shoulder strap supporting her lunch bag and a bronze hatchet. When she began hacking at the brush that had overgrown the trail, Bloch said:

"Here, let me!"

He drew from his gear an object the like of which Iroedh had never seen: a thing like a knife, but several times as large, with a straight back edge and a curved cutting edge that made the blade widest about a third of the distance from the point to the hilt. A single slash of this tool sent a swath of plants tumbling.

Iroedh started to exclaim in wonderment, then checked herself. She could not afford to risk the slightest advantage by impulsiveness. Her agile mind had instantly seen the possibilities of the thing as a weapon; in fact she wondered why none of the Avtini had thought of it. Bloch seemed to take it for granted that she was familiar with such a device, but if she made a fuss over it he would guess that she was not and invoke his precious regulations to keep her from learning more about it.

"What's your name for that?" she asked casually.

"A machete."

"*A matselh,*" she said, unconsciously giving the word the Avtinyk ending for tools and other artifacts.

"What would you call it?"

"A *valh,*" she replied, giving the Avtinyk for "knife." "Do you use them as weapons?"

Bloch paused before answering. "One could, though it's a little point-heavy for the purpose. Centuries ago we fought with implements like this, called 'swords.' The best shape for that use would be somewhat lighter and tapering to a narrow point. Now, however, we employ these." He touched the gun. "Or we should if we still had wars. How about your people?" he asked with a trace of suspicion.

"Oh, some Communities use them," Iroedh lied, "though the Avtini prefer the spear. May I try it?"

"Do not cut yourself," he warned, handing over the machete hilt-first.

Iroedh took a few awkward swipes at the brush before she got the hang of the tool. She gave an Avtiny smile as she imagined the next stalk to be the neck of an Arsuun of Tvaarm. *Swish!*

"Come on, come on," said O'Mara, who, with Barbe Dulac, had caught up with Bloch and Iroedh during the discussion. "Let a man be showing you how a trail is cleared."

And he waded into the brush with his own machete, sending great masses of vegetation flying.

Thereafter they took turns, all but Barbe Dulac, who

was too small. Sweat darkened the shirts of the three men until the two male ones pulled theirs off. Iroedh thereupon became fascinated by a Terran characteristic:

"Daktablak, how is it that though you say you're a functional male, you and O'Mara have rudimentary breasts like an Avtiny worker? Save that yours are even more rudimentary than ours."

"Your drones do not possess them?"

"No. Are you *sure* you're males?"

Bloch gave the barking Terran laugh. "I have always believed so."

She persisted: "And why doesn't the little Bardylak take off her tunic too? I should like to study her."

"It is against our custom."

At the request of Barbe Dulac, Bloch translated the last bit of conversation. Iroedh could not understand why Barbe turned red and O'Mara laughed loudly.

"These heathens have no shame at all," said the photographer, pausing to wipe the sweat from his forehead with the back of one hairy arm. "Here, Baldy," he said to Bloch, "take over."

Though Iroedh could catch only an occasional word, Bloch's manner told her he did not like to be so addressed. The xenologist went to work on the overgrowth in grim silence.

Iroedh dropped back to talk to Barbe Dulac, a process that entailed the usual difficulty when each knows but a few words of the other's language, though by pointing at things and making inquiring noises each soon expanded her vocabulary. The process was further complicated by the fact that the English spoken by the others was not Barbe's native tongue, for she came from a place she called Helvetia and the others Switzerland.

"We have the same sort of inconsistency," said Iroedh. "The Arsuuni call themselves *Arshuul,* but, as we have no *sh* sound and a different system of word endings, we call them *Arsuuni.*"

Then Iroedh took her turn at trail cutting, and the grade became too steep for conversation. They hoisted themselves over outcrops from which they could look far across the valley. For a time the trail wound along an almost sheer slope to which a few weeds clung precariously. Although the trail had been adequate when made, time and weather had piled debris on the cliffward side and worn away the outer edge so that they walked nervously along a reverse bank that almost spilled them over the

41

edge when the gravel rolled and slid away under their feet.

Iroedh pointed. "There's the ruin."

"If we live to see it," said O'Mara, mopping his forehead with his wadded-up shirt.

Another half hour brought them to the base of the shoulder on which the fortress stood, and from there it was an easy walk out. Bloch indicated the great blocks of Cyclopean masonry, weighing tons apiece, and asked:

"However did they transport their stones up here?"

Iroedh shrugged. "We don't know, unless they cut them from the cliff. The ancients did many things we can't duplicate."

"And when will we be eating?" said O'Mara.

"Any time," said Bloch.

They got out their lunch. Iroedh, munching her biscuits, asked about the various items of human food.

"Do you mean," she exclaimed, "that your males eat plant food and your females meat?"

"Yes, and the other way round," said Bloch. "Why don't you try a bite of meat?"

"Impossible! Not only is it against our laws, but when a worker has eaten nothing but plant food all her life a bite of meat would poison her. It's a painful death. Though it is said that thousands of years ago, before the reforms, people lived on such mixed diets, nowadays we should consider it a mark of savagery."

O'Mara produced a bottle filled with a yellow-brown liquid, which he unstoppered and drank from.

"Where'd you get that?" asked Bloch.

O'Mara grinned. "Out of Doc Markowicz's stores when the lad wasn't looking. Have a swallow."

He held out the bottle to Bloch, who hesitantly took it and drank.

"Weesky?" said Barbe Dulac. "Let me have some, please!"

"How about the native girl?" said O'Mara. "That's one human custom the darling should try."

"Be careful," said Bloch. "Just a sip. It might not agree with you."

Iroedh tipped her head back as she had seen the others do. Unaccustomed to drinking from such a vessel, she got a whole mouthful. She felt as if she had swallowed a bucket of live coals, and coughed violently, spraying half the mouthful on the ground.

"I—I'm poisoned!" she gasped between coughs.

"Let us hope not," said Bloch, thumping her back.

42

When Iroedh's equilibrium was restored he said: "Now let us prowl the ruins."

O'Mara replied: "You prowl, Baldy, while I take a bit of a snooze. The pictures wouldn't be no damn good with the sun so high anyway."

"I, too, should like to rest," said Barbe Dulac.

"How about you, Iroedh?" said Bloch.

Iroedh yawned, "Would you mind if I took a small nap also? I can hardly keep my eyes open."

"Do not tell me that half a swallow of whisky has had that much effect already!"

"I don't think it was that but the fact that I hardly slept last night."

"That is the coffee you drank yesterday. You nap, then, and I shall rouse you after a while."

O'Mara was taking another big swig and arranging his pack as a pillow. Barbe Dulac spoke to him:

"John, won't you get the sunburn, going to sleep with your chest bare?"

"Sure and these stinking little red dwarf stars don't put out enough ultraviolet to matter."

Iroedh asked for a translation, then inquired: "Is your sun, then, different from ours?"

"Very much so," said Barbe Dulac, "It looks about half as big and four times as bright. To us this one looks like a big orange—one of our fruits—in the sky."

"What do you call our sun?"

"Lalande 21185. That's just a number in a star catalogue."

Iroedh was about to ask what a star catalogue was when she saw that Barbe had dropped off. Accustomed to the simplest of sleeping accommodations, Iroedh dozed off herself, sprawled on the shattered pavement of the fort with her head pillowed on a stone.

Later the voices of the other two aroused her. While she struggled to remain asleep, she was brought sharply out of the twilight zone by a loud smack, as of an open hand striking bare flesh.

She opened her eyes to see Barbe Dulac stumble backward, half fall, and recover. A grille of red stripes across the female man's cheek implied that the sound *had* been that of a slap. Barbe screamed and O'Mara roared:

"That'll learn you to trifle with an honest man!"

He advanced with a curiously unsteady gait. Iroedh, gathering herself to rise, saw the bottle lying empty on the stones.

This conflict left Iroedh at a loss. She was sure it was

43

wrong, but as a member of another species she did not think it incumbent on her to intervene. At that moment, however, Bloch stepped around from behind a section of wall and walked toward O'Mara, saying:

"What's this? Look here, you can't——"

" 'Tis your doing!" cried O'Mara. "No bald-headed old omadhaun is going to steal my girl!"

Bloch halted in hesitation, his bodily attitude bespeaking fear of the other man's violence. He looked toward Barbe, who said something Iroedh could not catch. However, it seemed to stiffen his sinews, for he took another step toward O'Mara.

Smack! O'Mara's big fist shot out and struck the side of Bloch's face. Bloch's head snapped back and he fell supine upon the stones.

"Now," said O'Mara, "will you get up and fight like a man, or must I——"

Bloch got to his feet, moving at first slowly and jerkily, then with more agility. Iroedh, watching with horrified fascination, wondered why neither tried to pick up the gun or the machetes piled against the wall with the other gear. Such a method of settling differences was utterly foreign to the discipline of an Avtiny Community, where violence (except in war, the Royal Duel, and the Cleanup) was unknown.

With a roar O'Mara lowered his head and charged like a bull vakhnag. Bloch stood a fraction of a second holding futile fists before him, then threw himself to one side, leaving one long leg thrust out to trip his assailant. O'Mara tripped, staggered on in a half-falling run, and fetched up against the knee-high parapet that ran along a section of the cliffward side of the stronghold.

Iroedh had a glimpse of O'Mara's boots in the air, then—no O'Mara.

A long dwindling scream came up, cut off by the sound of a body striking a ledge. Sounds followed of the body striking again and again, and there was a rattle of loosened rocks.

"Tonnerre de Dieu!" said Barbe Dulac.

The three survivors hurried to the parapet and looked over. After they had searched for some seconds, Iroedh, catching a glimpse of contrasting color, said:

"Isn't that he in the branches of that khal tree?"

They looked where she pointed. Bloch got out a small black object with shiny glass eyes and looked through it.

"That is he," he said. "Dead, all right."

He handed the glasses to Iroedh. She almost dropped

them with astonishment as the pink-and-olive speck at the foot of the cliff leaped almost to within arms' length. After one long look she handed the glasses back.

"I'm sure he's very dead indeed," she said.

"I fear," said Iroedh, "I don't understand your Terran customs yet. Did the O'Mara leap off the cliff because of his love for Bardylak, or was that some sort of ceremonial execution?"

She stopped her questions when she saw the other two were paying no attention. They were jabbering at each other in their own tongue and Barbe Dulac was making strangled sounds while tears ran down her face. Iroedh understood this to be a Terran gesture symbolizing grief, but found it hard to understand. The female man had come to dislike O'Mara, who had certainly abused her. Why, then, such a display of emotion? Unless, of course, O'Mara was so important to the Terran Community that his death jeopardized its existence.

She caught an occasional word she knew, like "terrible" and "love." Presently the men put their arms around each other and pressed their mouths together, whereupon Barbe Dulac shed more tears than ever.

At last Bloch said to Iroedh: "You saw what occurred, did you not?"

"Yes, though I still don't understand it. Did O'Mara kill himself?"

"No. He was trying to kill me, or something close to it, and when I tripped him he fell over accidentally. Now, among us when one kills another for his own private purposes——"

"You mean as when we kill off surplus drones or defective workers for the good of the Community?"

"No; as if an Avtiny worker killed another merely because she disliked her, or because the other worker had something——"

"Such a thing could never happen!" Iroedh exclaimed.

"Your rogue drones attack workers to steal food and supplies, do they not?"

"That's different. A worker *never* attacks a fellow worker from the same Community, unless in carrying out the orders of the Council."

"It is different with us. The act is called 'murder' and is punished by death or long imprisonment."

"By 'long imprisonment' do you mean they starve the culprit to death? That's a strange——"

"No, they feed and house them, though not in fancy style."

"Then where's the punishment? Some of our lazier workers would like nothing better——"

Bloch made motions of tugging at his vanished hair. "We keep getting off the subject! Just permit me to talk, please. If I go back to the ship and narrate this incident as it happened, some will say I murdered O'Mara because of our rivalry over Barbe. And while I do not believe I should be convicted, since Barbe can testify it was an accident and self-defense, it would cause a great stench and ruin my reputation back on Terra——"

"If the death was justified according to your laws, why should anyone blame you?"

"Never mind; take it from me that my career would be jeopardized. Therefore Barbe and I will not mention any fight or slapping. We will simply say that he got intoxicated on the medicinal whisky and tried to show off by walking on the parapet, and fell over."

"You mean to *lie* to your own Community?"

"Not exactly; just to withhold part of the truth. He did get drunk and fall over the parapet, after all."

"A strange race, the men. What do you wish of me?"

"Not to spoil our story. Keep silent about the fight."

Iroedh pondered. "Would it be right?"

"We think so. I do not see what good would be accomplished by having an inquest and perhaps a trial when we were only defending ourselves."

"Very well, I'll say nothing. As I'm awake now, shall I explain the ruins to you?"

"Good God, no! We have to get back down, report O'Mara's fall, and endeavor to recover his body."

"Why? His clothes and equipment would be ruined by the fall."

"It is custom," said Bloch, starting to collect the gear.

"Do you eat the bodies of your dead? Or do you make soap of them as we do?"

Barbe Dulac squawked, and Bloch said: "Not ordinarily; we bury them ceremonially."

Iroedh sighed. "What people! Shall I carry his gear?"

Bloch gave Iroedh O'Mara's camera and container of photographic material and machete to carry, and led the way homeward. They wound down the trail, faster this time because it was mostly downhill and the worst brush had been cleared on the way up.

As she picked her way down with O'Mara's equipment banging against her skin as it swung from its straps,

Iroedh wondered on the predicament of her companions. While she liked them as individuals, as one might like a friendly ueg or other tame beast, her first loyalty still lay toward her Community. She would therefore not hesitate to turn their troubles to her own advantage if occasion offered.

She remembered the forgotten epic, the *Lay of Idhios*, which in its last canto told how the drone Idhios had used his knowledge of the liaison of Queen Vinir with the drone Santius to force the queen to steal the Treasure of Inimdhad and give it to him. That was back in the bad barbarous days when workers laid eggs and queens had but a single drone apiece, called the king, who presumed to dictate to the queen whom she should be fertilized by.

Evidently, in dealing with creatures of primitive social organization like the men or her own remote ancestors, one could sometimes extort goods and services from one by threatening to reveal something to her discredit. Could she force Bloch to help Elham against Tvaarm by threatening to tell Subbarau on him? For an instant she thought she had an answer to her Community's problem, and imagined Bloch mowing down the Arsuuny giants with his magical gun.

But then second thoughts dampened her enthusiasm. Bloch was not the head man in his Community. She could not use her knowledge to force the whole complement of the *Paris* to help Elham, because their leader was Subbarau, over whom she had no hold.

She might try to force Bloch to come back to Elham alone to fight for the Avtini—but that might not work either. Accustomed to a highly organized and disciplined Community, Iroedh realized that Bloch could probably not wander off at his own sweet will.

Another thought struck her. "Bardylak!"

"Yes?" said Barbe Dulac.

"Have you, in the sky ship, one of those machines that tells when a man is lying?"

"I understand we do. Nobody has to submit to it, but if an accused refuses, it makes the officers all the more suspicious."

So it wouldn't be necessary for Subbarau to find evidence of irregularities, but merely to have his suspicions aroused, and the true story of O'Mara's death would come out.

Then could she make Bloch reveal some bit of technical knowledge that would give the Avtini the advantage they needed? If, for example, he'd lend her the gun . . . A dubious expedient. The gun was a complicated mechanism, and if not used right might blow a hole in the user instead of the target. To tell the truth, Iroedh was definitely afraid of it. Besides, one needed a supply of the little brass things that went with it.

But something simpler, now, like the machete whose scabbard was slapping against her thigh. Anybody could understand that.

Then she remembered how the *Idhios* continued. As the triumphant Idhios turned away, his eyes upon the treasure in his hands, Queen Vinir had driven a knife into his back and slain him. She explained that Idhios had tried to fertilize her without her consent—an impossible situation under modern Community organization, but one that in ancient days, apparently, occurred often and was deemed a serious crime.

The lesson was that when you try to force a being of primitive social organization to do something for you by threatening to disclose her secret, take care she does not kill you to close your mouth forever.

However, if the *Lay* contained this warning, it also pointed the way out. For it transpired that Idhios had written an account of the relationship of Queen Vinir with Santius and left it with his friend Gunes with instructions to deliver it to King Aithles, the queen's one official drone, if anything happened to Idhios. So Gunes had given the tablet to the king, and the epic ended with King Aithles's minions holding Queen Vinir and her lover with their necks across the windowsill of the palace while the king hewed off their heads with a hatchet so that the heads fell into the moat.

Though as a result of her studies Iroedh was more broadminded than most Avtiny workers, even she could not visualize the slaying of a queen by a drone without a shudder. No wonder all the Avtiny Communities forbade the *Lay of Idhios!*

Would any such elaborate maneuver be necessary in her case, however?

They had nearly reached the floor of the valley of Gliid. Where the trail grew wider Bloch and Barbe Dulac walked side by side holding hands and paying Iroedh no heed.

While Iroedh had at first been a little irked at being ignored, she now began to calculate how to turn their absorption in each other to her advantage. She hefted the machete. Perhaps in the excitement of telling their story and organizing the search for O'Mara's body they'd never miss it.

She said: "Daktablak! If you like, I'll run ahead to our camp and ask our leader to assign some of us to help you recover the corpse."

"That will be splendid; thank you, Iroedh," said Bloch vaguely, and turned his attention back to Barbe.

Iroedh jogged off toward the main road, taking O'Mara's possessions with her.

IV. The Helicopter

At the Avtiny camp the only worker in sight was Vardh. Iroedh asked her:

"Where's Rhodh?"

Vardh pointed toward the towering bulk of the *Paris*. "Over there, prowling around in hope of picking up something useful. What sort of time have you had? Iinoedh thought they'd surely devour you——"

"Go fetch Rhodh, please, dear," said Iroedh.

Vardh went obediently. Iroedh walked over to her chariot, climbed up, and pulled up the seat cover, which was hinged and served as the top of a chest in which she stored her cloak and other gear. She wrapped the machete in the cloak and laid the bundle back in the recess, then closed the top and placed the camera and other things upon it.

"Well?" snapped Rhodh from the ground. "Will they fight on our side?"

Iroedh gave a jump; she had not expected Rhodh to slip up on her like that. Rhodh had removed her cuirass and kilt (though she still wore the hip-length haqueton-tunic) and so had been able to come close without clanking. Now was the time, before Bloch arrived, to show her the machete and explain her plans for duplicating it in bronze to use in battle.

"Not exactly," said Iroedh. "But I have——"

"What do you mean, not exactly? Will they fight for us or not?"

49

"No, but——"

"Failed again! I should have known better than to let you try. Another precious day wasted, with the Arsuuni due to march! I suppose that in your dreamy way you forgot all about our mission and spent your time discussing that rubbish on the Point! Of all the stupid, incompetent—— Anyway, I won't let it happen again. Tomorrow you can spend policing the camp while I take charge of Blok."

Rhodh marched off, leaving Iroedh to bite her lips. Forbidden thoughts of physical assault seeped into her mind, no doubt, she guessed, inspired by the lawless violence she had witnessed on Survivors' Point.

She called: "Rhodh!"

"What is it now?"

"I was trying to tell you one of the men fell off the cliff and was killed, and they'll want to fetch his body. You could ingratiate yourself with them by sending a party to help."

Rhodh glowered back. "Let the men tend to their own ridiculous customs and I'll tend to mine."

"Then I'll go——"

"You shall not! You shall clean the tethering area of the uegs and fetch them a fresh supply of greens. Get to work."

"Then you'd better return these to the men." Iroedh held up O'Mara's gear, all but the hidden machete. "They belong to the dead man, and the others will be looking for them."

"Hmp. Let me see them."

Rhodh took the articles and walked off, turning them over and pulling and poking at them. She walked toward the *Paris*, the low sun shining redly on the brass of her helmet.

Now, thought Iroedh, if the men start looking for the missing machete, O'Mara's goods will have passed through so many hands they'll never be able to establish responsibility for it.

Iroedh got out the shovel and went to work on the camp's least popular chore. Now she'd be cursed to the hell the ancient poems spoke of before she'd show Rhodh the machete. She would keep it hidden until she could find her own use for it.

"Iroedh darling!" said the voice of young Vardh. "Don't feel badly about Rhodh's harsh words. I'm sure you did the best you could, but she's in one of her worst humors. She's had a bad day too."

50

"What's happened?"

"This morning after brunch she decided to see the leader of the men. First she put on her armor, though the day was hot and the men don't seem to stand on much ceremony. But she told us to shut up; that she knew the right way for one leader to call upon another, and that men disapproved of nudity on formal occasions.

"Then she went over and tried to get the first man she saw to take her to that Sub—you know, the fat brown one, the leader. When the man didn't understand her she seemed to think she could make him understand by saying the same thing louder. Soon they were shouting, and the noise brought out the leader, who came down in the bucket to ask what was up. When he arrived Rhodh tried the same routine on him, with no more success. He indicated by sign language and his few words of Avtinyk that he was busy and she couldn't enter the ship because it was being cleaned or something, and back he went in the bucket.

"For a while she hung around watching the men. Some were scraping and painting the ship, which she could understand, but others were doing things that made no sense to her. Some were putting together that large magical device over there, the one with three petals sticking out from its top like a ripe pomuial. When she asked them what it was, one of them said something in his own language and flapped his arms like an ueg stallion in rut. So Rhodh thinks the device must have something to do with sex.

"Others brought out a round thing about so big"— Vardh held her hands about two feet apart—"and very light—so light that when one of them tossed it into the air it flew up into the sky while another man looked at it through a magical device. Others pulled up weeds, or turned over stones to catch the creeping things under them, which Rhodh says is a silly way for adults to act, though Avpandh thinks they may be short of food.

"One of them—the one with the almost-black skin and kinky hair—squatted in front of a box and turned little knobs on it, paying Rhodh no attention even when she spoke to him. After the third time with no response she prodded him in the buttocks with her spear. He leaped into the air with a yell and pointed a small *gon* at her, shouting in his own language. She gathered that he did not wish to be disturbed, and gave up trying to understand such unreasonable folk. She said the Terrans must have loaded all their crazy people into this ship and sent them off to get rid of them."

51

"She needn't take out her irritation on me," said Iroedh, proceeding determinedly with her work. She tried to make the sound Bloch had called whistling, but without success.

"Oh, you're right of course, darling," said Vardh. "Here, let me help you. Isn't is exciting, though? Like that oracular verse about

"When the gods descend from heaven's height
Shall the seed be sown.

You could call these sky folk the gods, and their magical knowledge the seed. If we could only persuade them to sow it!"

Iroedh said: "You're always quoting those things. As I remember, the quatrain begins with the line: 'When the Rogue Queen wears a crown of light,' which is utter nonsense. Whoever heard of a rogue queen? It's a contradiction in terms."

"Oh, I don't know. That little Terran female might be considered as such, since she seems to have no harem of drones of her own."

A noise around the *Paris* attracted their attention. Bloch and Barbe Dulac had returned. There was a mutter of Terran speech and much coming and going in the hoist. Rhodh's helmet towered amidst the crowd. Soon a group set out purposefully along the road toward Survivors' Point.

Iroedh finished her work and helped her juniors to prepare supper. Rhodh joined them for the meal. Nobody spoke much; Iroedh guessed that while the juniors sympathized with her, they did not dare show their feelings for fear of Rhodh's wrath. Vardh, however, made hers plain by sitting close to Iroedh and passing her everything before she was even asked to.

As they were washing up, the party that had set out for O'Mara's body returned with it. The three juniors dropped their jobs to rush across the camp to see.

Rhodh said in a low voice: "I'm sorry I spoke so harshly to you. Not but that you deserved chiding, but I let my petty emotions influence me. However, I still think it best if I deal with Blok tomorrow."

"It's nothing," said Iroedh, far from completely mollified. While Rhodh's sense of duty would force her to admit a patent mistake, that was not enough to make people like her. Rhodh continued:

"I do not mean to be hard on you, for at times you

52

display a glimmering of the qualities of a proper worker. If you would only model yourself on me, you might rise in the Community as I am doing."

"Thank you, but I'll continue to get along in my own inefficient way."

Iroedh stacked the last dish and walked off, knowing that by rejecting Rhodh's overture she had made an implacable enemy. But she could not force herself to truckle to one she now so disliked, as Rhodh would have done in her place.

Iroedh lay awake under her net, looking up at the stars through the meshes. Her mind roved in unaccustomed channels: If this was all the appreciation she got, why should she break her neck for her Community? Why not use her power to free Antis? Of course she would then have to do what she could for Elham, but Antis should come first. If that was anti-Communitarianism, let them make the most of it.

Now, what could Bloch do for Antis? He couldn't fly the *Paris* to Elham—at least not without the others' knowledge—and if she took him in her chariot he would be gone at least five days, which wouldn't do either. And when he got there, what? Not being even so strong as she, he could certainly not leap over the Community wall or batter down the stout gate. Perhaps he could blast it with his gun—but that would mean killing Elhamni, which Iroedh could not bring herself to contemplate.

For that matter, Bloch impressed her as a somewhat timorous creature—wise and likable, but no second Idhios. In fact, her early estimation of the Terrans as super-beings, impervious to the bodily ills and weaknesses of character that beset common mortals like herself, had been revised drastically downward as a result of the trip to the Point. Why, despite their science, they were in some respects even less godlike than the Avtini!

Half unconsciously she puckered her lips in one more effort to whistle. To her astonishment the sharp little sound rang out. She had to repeat it before she was sure it came from her own mouth.

She experimented. By moving her tongue back and forth, as Bloch had told her to do, she found she could vary the pitch. She tried to reproduce one of the few tunes she knew, that of the *Song of Geyliad,* which she had puzzled out from one of those manuscripts with the little black dots. The result might not have been recognized by the composer, but it pleased Iroedh.

"What's that funny noise?" came the sleepy voice of Avpandh.

"Some creeping thing," said the deeper tones of Rhodh. "Go to sleep."

Next morning Iroedh policed the camp until hardly a grass blade was out of place, then went to her chariot. From the chest containing the machete she took her writing tablet of vakhwil bark and wrote a concise account of the death of John O'Mara. She tore off and folded the top sheet, then sought out Vardh, who was gawking at the antics of the Terrans. Some of these were repairing pieces of machinery with magical devices that sparkled and shone.

"Come with me," said Iroedh. "Can you keep a secret, Vardh dearest?"

"For you? Certainly!"

"Even from Rhodh?"

Vardh looked around nervously, but Rhodh was off somewhere with Bloch. "Especially from her. Though she's our leader, I don't really like her!"

"Even from the Council?"

Vardh's eyes widened and her slit pupils dilated. "O-oh, this must be something simply awful! But for you I would."

"Even from the queen?"

Vardh hesitated. "N—yes, I would. Not one of them is so nice as you. I love you almost as well as I do the Community."

Iroedh handed her the folded sheet. "This is what you must do: Hide this message, without looking at it, in your chariot. Should anything happen to me, like death or imprisonment, see it gets into the hands of Captain Subbarau. That is, if the sky ship is still here, or if I haven't asked for the sheet back. And not a word to anybody!"

"I understand, darling," said Vardh.

She hurried off. Iroedh approached the ship, where several men were putting the finishing touches on the machine with the "petals" that Rhodh had observed. Barbe Dulac stood there, alternately looking at the machine and at something on her finger.

"May I see that?" said Iroedh.

Barbe held up her left hand. For the first time Iroedh became really conscious of the fact that men had one more digit on each extremity than the Avtini. On the third finger sparkled a faceted gem, like those the ancients used to make, held in place by a slender ring of gray metal.

54

"Winston gave it to me," said Barbe.

"What?"

They struggled with each other's languages until Iroedh understood and replied: "That was kind of him, wasn't it?"

"Oh, more than that! It means we are engaged to be married!"

"You mean one of those Terran mating contracts?"

Barbe sighed. "Yes. The silly darling brought it all the way from Earth, but did not dare say anything because he was afraid of John O'Mara. He is a timid old rabbit, that one, but I love him even if he has no hair."

"That is nice."

"You have no idea! It is too bad you people do not have the love as we know it."

"Thank you, but if your kind of love makes people throw each other off cliffs, I'm satisfied with ours. By the way, when will you be fertilized? I should like to know how it is done."

Barbe emitted a sound of strangulation, followed by coughs and gasps, meanwhile turning almost as red as an Avtin. Iroedh, not knowing what she could have done to cause such a reaction, assumed Barbe had gotten something in her windpipe.

Barbe straightened up and said: "Look! Kang is almost ready to take off!"

"To take off what? His clothes?"

"No, the helicopter."

"The hil—hiila——I meant to ask you, what is that thing for?"

"It flies."

"It what?"

"Flies through the air." Barbe made motions.

"Oh, now I see why Rhodh thought it was concerned with sex! Can all of you men drive it?"

"No. Kang will not let anybody but himself and Winston fly it."

The little black-haired man with the flat yellow face got into the machine, and the men who had been working on it scattered.

Iroedh said: "Daktablak flies it?"

"He is a good flier, him."

"He must be brave after all."

"In some ways. The flying machines and the high places and the savage animals do not bother him, but any man who shouts at him can make him fold up. I shall have to supply the spine he lacks."

"The poor man has bones missing? He seems very active for a cripple——"

Before Barbe could straighten out Iroedh again, the helicopter coughed and whirred. The petals spun faster and faster until their down draft blew clouds of dust radially outward into the faces of the spectators. Iroedh and Barbe backed up until they were out of the sand-storm. They stood watching the rotors, while Kang made his interminable adjustments, and struggled with the speech barrier. Iroedh found that, while Terran grammar and vocabulary came easily enough, she could not exactly imitate the men's pronunciation, because her vocal organs differed from theirs.

"What," said Iroedh, "do you call this world?"

"We have named it 'Ormazd,' and the two uninhabited planets of this system 'Mithras' and 'Ahriman' after the gods of an ancient Terran religion."

"Why don't you use our own name?"

"What is it?" asked Barbe.

"We call it 'Niond.'"

"Does that mean 'earth' or 'soil'?"

"Why yes! How did you know?"

"That is usually the case. Do all Communities call it by the same name?"

"No. With the Arsuuni it is 'Sveik.'"

"Well, there you are. We might as well pick a name of our own as try to decide among those in use here."

The burbling whistle of the blades speeded up. The wind increased and the helicopter rose gently. Kang hov-ered a bit, then climbed until he was a mere speck and set off on a circuit of the valley.

Iroedh asked: "How fast does that thing go?"

Barbe shrugged. "Perhaps two hundred kilometers an hour. I do not know what that would be in your measure-ments, but it is ten or twenty times the speed you can run."

"Can it carry more than one?" Iroedh tried to calculate how long the round trip to Elham would take.

"It has room for three, and can lift an even greater weight."

"Do you think I could ride in it?"

Barbe looked wide-eyed at her companion. "You would not have fear?"

"If it can carry you men it will carry me; and anyway I feel lucky. Could I?"

"I should have to ask. They do not let Kang take us on

what they call joy rides, because the fuel is limited. But you as a native of this world might be a special case. There is Lobos, the executive officer; I will ask him."

Iroedh watched, impassive outside but excited within, as her little human friend conversed with a small dark man, and both went to speak to Subbarau, who had likewise been a spectator.

Barbe reported: "They say it will be all right if Kang thinks it safe."

Kang grew from a speck into a whirligig and thence into a helicopter settling down on his take-off spot. When he shut off the engine Barbe ran over to the machine and spoke to him; then beckoned Iroedh.

The flat face grinned invitingly through the open door. Iroedh climbed in and settled herself as he directed her, but fumbled with her safety belt till he fastened it for her.

Up they went. Iroedh, seeing the ground fall away, gripped her armrests until her knuckles faded from red to pale pink, the same terrible fear sweeping over her as in the hoist. She set her jaws, determined not to lose her brunch or otherwise disgrace her race before these formidable aliens.

"You like?" said Kang.

Iroedh forced herself to open her eyes and look out through the transparent covering of the machine. Little by little the heart-stopping fear subsided. She found herself looking down upon the shiny nose of the *Paris*, the whole sky ship appearing no bigger than one of the pins used in *uintakh*. Fear surged back with the thought that Kang might, with the unpredictability of Terrans, throw her out of the machine. But her good sense fought down the idea. If they had wanted to kill her they could have done so more easily. She stretched her lips in a smile—not her own kind, but the Terran tooth display that reminded her of a noag about to bite.

"I—I—like," she said.

The ground now looked like a relief map, the people mere specks. The fear went away. Mount Wisgad smoked quietly in the distance.

She asked in her fumbling English: "Can you down—lower—string—rope—for man up climb?"

"Sure thing. Can haul three, four men up at once. Very strong machine. Made by Vought—damn good company."

Little by little a plan for rescuing Antis took form.

Iroedh spent the afternoon studying an English primer

Bloch had left with Barbe to give to her. Rhodh returned well before supper in an even worse humor than before, refusing to speak to anyone. The sun was setting when Iroedh slipped out of the Avtiny camp and went purposefully over to the *Paris*.

Bloch was pacing about the base of the space ship, holding a curious object in his teeth, something like a small spoon with a deep scoop-shaped bowl. A curl of smoke rose from the bowl.

Iroedh said: "Hail, Daktablak! Do you then breathe fire like the monster worm Igog in the *Tale of Mantes?*"

"No." He explained the uses of tobacco.

"Have you quarreled with Rhodh? She's in a remarkable rage, even for her."

"Not exactly. She and I are not—how would you say it?—congenial. We experienced the same difficulty when she was here previously."

"What happened today?"

"Well, first she talked too rapidly for me to comprehend her, and took it as an insult when I requested her to slow down. Then she proposed a deal to me: If I would intervene in your fool war, she would try to arrange for us to visit her Community, if her Council would assent. Did you tell her I had tendered such a proposal?"

"No," said Iroedh.

"She seemed to think I had, and when I endeavored to explain why I could not she lectured me, waving her spear in my face, until I politely informed her I had my own work to do. And when I tried to collect some information from her she became uncommunicative. Well, it was altogether a pretty sticky day."

"I'm told you can drive the flying machine."

"That is correct."

"And that the machine can lift several people from the ground by means of a rope."

"Yes. In fact there is a rope ladder coiled up in a compartment in the bottom for rescue work. You push a lever and it falls out."

"It would be bad for you if Captain Subbarau heard the complete story of the death of O'Mara, wouldn't it?"

"Ssh! I thought we weren't going to mention that?"

"Not if you do what I ask."

"What is this? Blackmail?"

"If that's what you call it. I don't wish to do it, but I must to save my friend Antis."

"Who is that? A drone, from his name."

58

Iroedh told about Antis, adding: "And don't think to make away with me, because I've written an account of the fight and arranged for it to be shown Subbarau should anything befall me."

"Bless my soul! And I thought you Ormazdians were too primitive and innocent to think of angles like that! You do not really mean this?"

"I certainly do."

There followed a long argument. Bloch appealed to all Iroedh's sentiments—honor, friendship, and so on—without budging her. When she felt herself weakening she thought of Antis being speared like a fish at the next Cleanup.

"One would think," said Bloch bitterly, "you were in love with this Antis, in our Terran sense."

"What a revolting idea! Love between workers and other beings has nothing to do with sex."

"What do you wish me to do?"

"Are you on guard tonight?"

"Until midnight," he said.

"Then I wish you to take me in the flying machine to Elham and rescue the imprisoned drones by means of that rope ladder. If the machine is as fast as it's said to be we can be back by midnight."

"How am I supposed to deliver them if they're in some subterranean prison cell?"

"Ah, but they're not! The cell where imprisoned drones are kept is in the top of the queen's dome, with a walkway running around it for the guard."

"How do you gain access to the cell from there?"

"There's a window, small, but big enough to squeeze through, covered by bronze bars. I've hauled my spear and buckler around the walkway often enough to know it."

"Well, that settles it. You could not expect me to gnaw through the bars with my teeth, could you?"

"You men have magical cutting devices that cut through metal as though it were water. I saw the men using them today."

"You seem to think of everything. How can we locate the place at night? It will not look at all familiar."

"We shall follow the coast of the Scarlet Sea to Khinad Point. I know that coast well."

"How about the guard?"

"Leave her to me. In another hour everybody will be asleep and it will be dark. I'll meet you here, and you shall have with you one of those magical cutting devices. Farewell for the nonce, Daktablak."

"Damn you, Iroedh," he muttered at her retreating back.

V. The Queen's Dome

As the helicopter soared over Khinad Point, Iroedh pointed inland to where the pale domes of Elham, like a cluster of eggs, showed among the fields and woods.

"That's where we go," she said.

"You have remarkable night vision," said Bloch. "I cannot see the thing at all. It must be those split pupils."

He swung the machine toward their objective. After a few minutes Iroedh could make out the wall of the Community, like the rim of a wheel whose hub was the cluster of domes.

Under Iroedh's guidance he spiraled down upon the domes. She pointed:

"That big one in the middle is the queen's dome. Do you see that circle near its top? That's the guard's walkway. That dark spot just above the circle is the window of the condemned drones' cell. Do you see it?"

"Yes."

"Then lower your ladder and I'll climb down it."

"Get your legs out of the way. There, up on the crossbar. And watch your landing; it's a windy night."

Bloch pushed a knob. There was a mechanical sound beneath them, audible over the purr of the motor and the swish of the blades, and a trap door dropped open where Iroedh had been resting her feet. Leaning forward she could see down through the trap door into empty space, in which the top two or three rungs of the rope ladder could be perceived jerking about in the air stream.

With a prayer to Gwyyr, Iroedh thrust a leg down into the opening and felt for the fixed rung; then the other leg. At last she located the topmost ladder rung and lowered her weight down upon it. Before she knew it she was altogether below the helicopter, clutching the swaying support, her cloak whipping and swirling about her as the helicopter rocked in the gusts.

Fear of falling gripped her so that she could hardly make herself look down, or let go a rung to shift her grip to the next. As she mastered her feelings she saw that the machine was descending rapidly toward the top of the queen's dome, at such an angle that the path of the lower end of the ladder would be tangent to the circular walkway.

Iroedh quickly lowered herself the rest of the length of the ladder. Over the noise of the helicopter she heard the tweedle of flute music and a voice:

"Ho there! Who are you?"

The guard was standing on the walkway a few feet from where Iroedh would strike it, her spear at ready, her helmeted head tilted back. Although it was too dark to recognize her by starlight, Iroedh knew that the guard's face must wear an astonished expression.

While reason told her it was but a matter of seconds, it seemed a year before the hovering helicopter brought her into position. She swung off the ladder, fell a couple of feet, and landed lightly in a crouch. Her hands flew to her throat to untie the cord that held her cloak in place.

For this cloak was her only weapon. Not wishing Bloch to know she possessed O'Mara's machete, and not wishing to add murder to her other offenses against the Community, she intended to attack the guard by the *rumdrekh*. As the spear darted out, one whipped one's cloak around it and jerked it out of the hands of the foe, dropped the cloak, reversed the spear, and went into action in the normal manner.

"Who goes there?" cried the guard over the sound of the wind.

As Iroedh rose to her feet without answering, holding her cloak in her hands, the guard's spear fist went up and back for the overhand stabbing thrust. The spearhead shot out. Iroedh whirled her cloak and felt the point of the spear foul itself in the folds. She tried to give that extra flip and jerk that guaranteed success, at the same time reaching with her free hand for the spear shaft . . .

But this guard was no tyro, and one of the biggest workers of the whole Community of Elham. With dismay Iroedh felt the cloak jerked entirely from her grasp as the guard pulled her spear back. Another jerk sent the cloak flying away on the wind. The guard took a long step forward, her burnished greaves glistening faintly in the starlight, and drew back her arm for another thrust. This one would not miss.

In theory an agile worker, so attacked, had a remote chance of seizing the spear shaft and wresting it from her assailant. Iroedh, now entirely unencumbered except for the magical cutting device strapped to her side, had whatever meager advantage that fact gave her. In practice, however, she realized that her luck had now run out. If one snatched the spear too soon, one caught the head and severed the tendons of one's fingers on its edges; if too late, the spear point would already have reached one's vitals.

At least, she thought in the last flash, once you were dead nothing hurt any more. And since her mission had obviously failed, Antis would die, and life without him would hardly be worth the bother. She winced, closing her eyes, as the spear head darted forward.

But no point tore into her viscera. When she opened her eyes it was to see the guard drop her spear with a clatter and turn to run. The noise and wind of the helicopter had greatly increased, so that the down-wash tore at Iroedh's bare body as if it would hurl her from the walkway down the slippery slope of the dome.

Gwyyr must have heard; Bloch, bless his alien hearts, had brought his machine around in a tight circle and swooped so close to the dome that the alighting gear almost touched the combatants.

Clang! went the shield of the guard on the stones: one of the big bronze bucklers used for guard mount, ornamental, but too heavy for field use. The guard headed for the stair that spiraled down the lower half of the dome from the walkway.

"Hurry up!" called Bloch from the open window of his aircraft.

Iroedh sprinted around the walkway, her bare feet making no sound against the noise of the helicopter and the clatter of the guard descending the stairs. Meanwhile her hand sought the cutting device at her waist.

A quarter of the way around she came to the window of the drones' cell.

"Antis!" she called softly.

"For the love of Dhiis, is that you, Iroedh?" came the familiar voice. "What on Niond is going on, and how did you get here? I thought you were at Gliid!"

"No time to explain. Are you and the others ready to escape?"

"We should love to—but how?"

"Leave that to me. Stand back!"

Iroedh felt the cutting device until she found the stud that actuated it. She pressed the button and a thin line of light appeared along the edge near the end. She touched this edge to one of the bars at its upper end. With a shower of sparks the instrument sheared through the thick bronze as if it had been tarhail mush.

Bloch had warned her not to touch the edge to her own person, lest she be similarly sectioned. An "electronic knife," he had called it, which meant nothing to her.

Below, she could hear the voice of the guard shouting the alarm. *Zzip!* went another bar, and then the third. Iroedh withdrew the instrument and applied it to the lower ends of the bars. *Zzip! Zzip! Zzip!* Two of the bars tumbled in through the slanting window to fall with a clatter to the floor of the cell. The third struck with a soft thump, followed by an outburst of dronish bad language: ". . . the fertilizing thing landed on my toe!"

Iroedh put the instrument back in its case and said: "Can you climb out now?"

"Don't know," said Antis. "One of us will have to boost another up."

With much male grunting, Antis's head and shoulders appeared in the opening.

"Give me a hand, beautiful," he said.

Iroedh pulled, and out he came asprawl on the walkway. As he rose to his feet, the forepart of Kutanas appeared, to be helped out likewise.

Below in the courts Iroedh could hear the clink of arms and the voice of the guard talking excitedly with unseen persons. Any minute a party would come storming up the stair.

Kutanas and Antis reached back into the darkness of the cell to seize the wrists of Dyos and pull him up. When he was half out of the window he got stuck.

"The stumps of those bars are disemboweling me!" he complained.

"Shall we leave him?" said Iroedh, who did not care much what happened to Dyos so long as Antis was saved.

"I should say not!" said Antis. "We drones have to stick together. Brace your foot, Kutanas, and heave!"

"I told him not to eat so much," grunted Kutanas. "Ready?"

They heaved, and Dyos came like a tooth being plucked from its socket.

"Ow! Ow!" lamented Dyos, rubbing the scraped parts. "I shan't be able to sit for days."

From below came the unmistakable sound of a party of armed workers, and their officer's voice: "One at a time, and hold your spears at ready . . ."

"Daktablak!" called Iroedh loudly into the darkness.

"Here," said Bloch, swinging the helicopter back toward the window.

Dyos flinched as the machine swooped close, and seemed about to run. Antis exclaimed:

"What in the name of Tiwinos is that?"

"Never mind. When I climb the rope ladder that hangs down from it, you do likewise. I shall climb into the machine, but you three hold your places on the ladder while the machine lifts you over the wall and sets you down outside."

"I'm afraid!" wailed Dyos.

"Stay behind and be butchered then," snapped Iroedh. She caught the lashing ladder on the third try and began her climb.

The clatter of the guards came clearly over the sounds of the wind and the helicopter. From her height Iroedh could see them coming up the stair, spears ready. Directly below her, Antis scrambled up, and below him the other two. She reached the machine, too excited to feel fear, and swung into the swaying cabin.

"Go!" she said to Bloch.

Bloch did things with his levers and the aircraft rose. A chorus of exclamations came up from the guards as they rushed to the spot from which Dyos had just been lifted. A couple threw their spears at him, but he was already too high. The spears fell back upon the stonework and went rolling and rattling down the sides of the dome.

As Iroedh settled into her seat, Antis thrust his crest up through the trap door. "What now?"

She replied: "We'll drop you in the tarhail field outside the wall. When you get to the woods north of this field, you'll have cover almost all the way to the Lhanwaed Hills. Watch the road from Thidhem, and when I get back from Gliid I'll meet you at Khinam. I shall make this sound——"

She whistled a bar of the refrain of the *Song of Geyliad*.

"How do you do that?" he asked.

"I'll teach you when we have time. We're past the wall; get ready to drop."

Antis spoke to Kutanas below him as the helicopter sank toward the field. It occurred to Iroedh that the agricultural officer would have a fit when she found that a great swath had been trampled in her ripe grain.

64

Dyos dropped off, but stupidly failed to get out from under Kutanas, so that the latter came down on top of him and both rolled in the dirt. Antis landed on his feet, called up: "Farewell, beautiful!" and ran for the woods at the north side of the field, crying for the others to follow.

"Now," said Iroedh, "take me home. . . . Oh, *prutha!*"

"What is it?"

"I left my cloak on the dome where the guards will surely find it."

"Has it got your name on it?"

"No, though I should know it anywhere by the tears I've mended. But when I return to the camp without a cloak, and the word gets around that an unclaimed one was found at the scene of the rescue, some busybody will put the facts together. Still, we dare not go back for it; that would be pressing our luck too far."

"Tell them you gave it to Barbe in exchange for one of her feminine doodads. I will see that she gives you one."

Rhodh asked: "Last night I am sure I heard the flying machine of the men go up and come down again later. Do you know anything about it, Iroedh?"

"Not a thing, Leader," said Iroedh, patting her biscuits into shape.

"Well, I am not satisfied with the situation. You are all confined to the camp for the day; I do not wish you to become involved with these dangerous and immoral creatures."

Iroedh and the three juniors exchanged wordless looks. Rhodh strapped on her kilt and cuirass, wriggled her head into her helmet, took up her spear, and walked off toward the *Paris*.

Iroedh went back to her chores, but presently looked up to see Barbe Dulac bearing down upon her. The female man held a small gold-colored box in her extended hand, and said in a voice evidently meant for all within earshot:

"Here you are, Iroedh dear. And thank you again for the lovely cloak."

"What's that?" said Vardh.

"Oh," said Barbe, "Iroedh and I are exchanging gifts, products of our respective worlds."

"That little thing for a cloak?" said Iinoedh in wonderment. "What does it *do?*"

"We Terran females use it to give ourselves the beauty," said Barbe.

"How?" inquired Avpandh.

Barbe opened the little box. "First, here is a—how would you say mirror?"

While this was being cleared up the Avtini crowded around to look at their reflections. Iroedh, though familiar with the mirror of polished brass used by the queen to prepare herself for the visits of her drones, was astonished by the fidelity of the image in the compact. It was like looking through a tiny window into another world.

"Now there is this," said Barbe, pulling out a small furry disk. "It is called a powder puff. Among us a shiny nose is considered ugly. Hold still, Iroedh."

Barbe applied the furry disk with small dabs to Iroedh's nose. Iroedh inhaled a breath of powder and sneezed.

Barbe said: "Now comes the lipstick. Make your mouth like so ... You really need a darker shade, because your skins are almost as red as this already."

Barbe stood back from her handiwork. The three juniors looked at Iroedh and whooped with mirth.

Barbe screwed up her face at the sound and asked: "What is that noise? It sounds like a Terran creature called an owl."

The young Avtini explained that the hooting sound was merely their version of laughter, and insisted that Barbe do likewise by them. Vardh said:

"What's it supposed to do, to color our faces like this? Do you prepare for some ceremonial in this manner?"

"You might say so," said Barbe. "This is how one catches a male."

"You mean as when we round up surplus drones to kill them at the Cleanups?"

"No; a much more agreeable ceremony."

As the juniors straggled off to resume their tasks, Barbe said to Iroedh in a lower voice: "Winston told me about your expedition last night. That was naughty of you, Iroedh."

"I know, but what could I do? Is he still angry with me?"

"He was at first, that you should have made him risk his life on something that was none of his affair. But I thought I should do the same if he were in prison, and that he should have had enough romance in his soul to take the risk without having to be blackmailed into it. I told him he was a spineless old rabbit with no sentiment, caring nothing for anything but his scientific records and the good opinions of his superiors in the government department he works for. So now he is all subdued, that one."

"What is this 'romance' and 'sentiment' you talk about? Has it something to do with your special Terran kind of love?"

"A great deal. It is hard to explain, but—— I know; can you read English?"

"A little. I know what sounds the letters stand for, and I can puzzle out simple passages."

"It is good the English speakers reformed their spelling not many years ago, because before then it was so irregular you could never have mastered it. What I am getting at is that I will give you a Terran book I brought to Ormazd."

"You're much too kind!" cried Iroedh.

"No, no, I have finished it. They do not like one to take bound books on the ship anyway, because of the weight. Their library is all photographed down small on little cards that one reads with an enlarging machine, but I like to read in bed and one cannot hold the machine on one's lap in the bunk, so I brought a real book."

"What's in this book?"

"No scientific information, but it will tell you what we mean by the 'romance' and the 'sentiment.'"

"What is it called?"

"*A Girl of the Limberlost,* by an American writer named Porter. It was first published hundreds of years ago, but for some reason was reprinted recently, and I happened to come upon a used copy in a bookstall in Genève. As it is the most sentimental story I have ever read, I think you will find it interesting."

Later in the day Rhodh returned, took one look, and cried: "What in the name of Eunmar have you been doing to your faces?"

When Vardh stammered an explanation, Rhodh said: "That is enough! Wash off that filth! I see you cannot be trusted anywhere near these men, who will corrupt you with their degenerate customs. We leave for Elham at once."

"What!" cried Iroedh. "But we haven't finished with the men—or they with us——"

"We have indeed finished with them. I interviewed them again this morning and found them absolutely adamant against helping us."

"But they wish to learn about our world——"

"For what purpose? So they can conquer it more easily? You always were a credulous fool, Iroedh. In any case, they can learn from some other Community; we are all

67

needed back home to help in the war with Tvaarm. Strike the camp and pack your gear right away."

Iroedh got to work folding the stove and hitching up the uegs. In less than an hour they were lined up.

"Ready?" barked Rhodh.

She cracked her whip and they got into motion, the uegs pulling on the shafts with their big knobby hands. As they reached the main road through the valley of Gliid, Iroedh turned right toward the *Paris* instead of left toward Thidhem.

"Ho there!" shouted Rhodh. "You have mistaken your turn, Iroedh!"

Iroedh called back: "No, I'm going to speak to one of the men. Go on; I shall catch up."

"Come back here!" screamed Rhodh. "You shall do no such thing!"

Iroedh, as if she had not heard, kept right on.

A quarter-hour later she caught up with the tail of the procession, happy in the knowledge that the Terran book lay snug at the bottom of her chariot chest along with O'Mara's machete. Rhodh, leading the column, kept her helmeted head rigidly to the front, as if she were unaware of Iroedh's presence.

When they came to a wide stretch Vardh reined back alongside Iroedh and told her softly: "You know, Iroedh darling, I don't think she's leaving because of the attitude of the men at all. We might have accomplished much in a few more days."

"What, then?"

"She's made a fool of herself by antagonizing them, so she cannot bear the scene of her mistakes. And she can't let you represent us any more because if you succeeded you'd get the credit."

Iroedh said: "I was always taught to put the good of the Community before my own glory. Rhodh used to be as pleasant as any other worker before she became consumed with ambition."

"Isn't it true? They say she plans to run for foreign officer at the next election. Why don't you run against her? We'd all vote for you."

"By Gwyyr, such a thought never occurred to me! You want these bustling characters, interested in every petty detail, on the Council, not an impractical antiquarian dreamer like me."

The five members of the mission to Gliid drove back to Elham in an all-day rain. Iroedh, when her ueg had been

68

turned back to the Community stables, went to her quarters. In the recreation room of her section she found some of her friends and asked them if Tvaarm had begun its expected invasion yet.

"Not yet," said Tydh, resting after a night of guard duty. "But it's been just as exciting as if they had."

"How so?"

"Haven't you heard of the disappearance of the condemned drones? But of course, you've been out of touch with Elham. During the night a great black flying thing came down upon the queen's dome, tore open the bars of their cell, snatched them out, and flew away with them. The guard on dome duty told how she attacked the monster with her spear, but it knocked her halfway down the stair with a flick of its legs."

Iroedh noticed that the guard's account made no mention of a human adversary. No doubt the poor guard had not cared to confess her flight.

"And the funniest thing was," continued Tydh, "that the cloak of an Avtin was found on the dome alongside the walkway. The guards who rushed up the dome just as the monster flew away all swear they weren't wearing any, and the drones had no clothing in their cell. It's a great mystery."

Iroedh's hearts pounded. Tydh went on:

"It's just like the old legends in which gods like Tiwinos and Dhiis came down to Niond to right wrongs and fertilize mortals. In fact, some of the workers are talking of reviving the ancient religion."

"That sounds like fun. What does the Council say?"

"Oh, they tell us not to be silly. And another thing: The Council has set the Royal Duel for five days from today!"

"Really?"

"Yes. I'm offering three to one on Estir, if you care to lay a bet. Eiudh is trying to wangle a mission to Ledhwid so she can ask the Oracle to predict the outcome and clean the rest of us out, while Gruvadh is going through all the prophetic quatrains to find one that fits the case, and Ythidh spends all her liberty upon the domes watching the flight of flying things for omens."

"How does Intar take it?"

"The queen is furious. She says it's a conspiracy to get rid of her, and that if her fertility is down it's only because of the poor quality of the drones the Council has furnished her."

Iroedh grew cold inside. She was sure she could somehow combine her possession of the machete with the impending accession of Estir to her own advantage, but could not think how. She would have to act quickly, because when Rhodh learned about the mysterious abandoned cloak she would probably remember the flight of the helicopter on the night the drones disappeared, and draw the natural inference.

Tydh said: "How about a game of uintakh?"

"No, thank you. The Terrans lent me a book which I'm mad with curiosity about."

Iroedh excused herself and went to her private cell for the book. As she did not have to report for work until the following morning she settled herself comfortably in the recreation room for a good long read, evading the pleas of her friends to join them in practicing the figures of round dances to be danced at the forthcoming Queens' Conference.

She found the book hard going, for despite the exceptional linguistic talent for which she was known in the Community her knowledge of English was not so good as she had thought. While some unfamiliar words she could guess from context or infer from the primer Bloch had given her, others, like "daffy" or "calico," left her baffled. Still, the general story line of *A Girl of the Limberlost* was reasonably clear, making allowance for the strangeness of Terran culture and customs.

She was deeply immersed in the adventures of Elnora Comstock when a voice said: "Oh, Iroedh dear!"

Iroedh looked up to see the agricultural officer standing over her.

"I have bad news for you," continued the councilman.

Iroedh's hearts skipped a beat. Had they discovered her guilt in the matter of the disappearing drones already? She sat as if paralyzed.

The agricultural officer said: "Rhodh presented her report to us as soon as she got in. Well, you know Rhodh. She made much of the difficulties she worked under, and of the coldly unfriendly attitude of the men, and of the incompetence and insubordination of her juniors—especially one Iroedh. In fact, she demanded that your efficiency rating be reduced.

"Of course we know Rhodh is simply eaten with ambition to be the next foreign officer, and is trying to cover up her failure to get help from the men. At least I know it, though I couldn't make the rest of the Council see it. She has friends in high places, it seems, and one must admit she works herself to a frazzle for the good of the

70

Community. Anyway, they commended her and docked your rating by five points. I'm so sorry, my dear!"

Iroedh let out her breath. So *that* was all! Ordinarily she would have been furious at such unjust treatment, but now the agricultural officer's words came as a relief.

"I've survived worse things," she said. "But thank you for what you tried to do."

Tired of reading, she went back to her cell to plan her next move. She wanted to see Antis and show him the machete, now hidden under her pallet. She had brought it into her cell wrapped in her net. She could of course wrap it in her net again, but if anyone saw her going out with a net under her arm they might well wonder why she was going to spend the night outside the Community. What she most urgently needed was a new cloak.

She filled out a requisition for a new cloak from stores, all but the signature, and took the bark sheet and the Terran make-up kit Barbe Dulac had given her to the queen's apartments. As it was not yet laying time she had no difficulty getting in. She presented the compact to the queen and explained its use.

"For me?" said Intar. "Thank you, my good Iroedh. Do you know, you're the only member of that group that went to Gliid who remembered to bring me a present?"

"It's nothing, Queen. However, there is one small matter. I traded my cloak for that kit, and should like you to initial this requisition for a new one."

"Certainly." Queen Intar scrawled her initials on the bottom of the sheet and handed it back. "Of course I'm not supposed to have opinions about such matters, my dear, but I think it was a shame that the Council commended Rhodh and disciplined you."

Iroedh took the requisition to stores and drew a new cloak. Toward sunset she got a take-out meal from the section mess and set out afoot for Khinam, the machete wrapped in the cloak and the cloak under her arm.

She settled herself in the section of the ruins where she and Antis had so often picnicked. While she was setting out her supper she whistled the *Song of Geyliad*.

"Here we are, beautiful!" cried a voice, and Antis dropped laughing from the top of the ruined wall.

Iroedh jumped up with a little shriek of startlement. They threw their arms around each other and squeezed, then held each other at arms' length. Iroedh noted that Antis had lost weight and had acquired a hollow-eyed

71

look; also that he was wearing an Avtiny worker's cloak and boots.

"Where did you get those?" she asked.

"Ask me no questions and I'll tell you no lies. You didn't by chance bring any *meat,* did you?"

"No. I thought of it, but if I went to the royal mess and asked for it they'd wonder what I wanted it for."

"I suppose so," he said in a less enthusiastic tone. "What couldn't I do to a nice juicy leipag steak!"

"Haven't you eaten since the rescue?"

"Practically nothing. You forgot you dropped us in that field as naked as the day we were hatched, without even boots. My feet are somewhat hardened from coming out with you, but Dyos and Kutanas have had a rough time."

"Couldn't you make yourself a bow and arrows to hunt your meat with?"

"What with? You need a tool of some sort. I left Kutanas back in the woods trying to scrape a sapling into a spear with a sharp stone, but at the present rate we shall all be dead before he finishes it. We tried to get into the leipag enclosure to steal one, but no luck; it was too well guarded. Yesterday I caught a hudig with my bare hands, but that gave us only one good bite apiece."

"You poor fellows! Take this, then," she said, handing over her knife. "You can at least carve bows and spears with it."

"Thanks. This isn't really good hunting territory, because the workers of Elham and Thidhem have killed off or driven away most of the game so that rogues like us shall have no source of food save dhwygs and other creeping things." He looked hungrily at Iroedh as she ate her biscuits and vegetables. "I'd even eat that mess of yours if I didn't mind dying in convulsions."

"Would you like to get back into the Community?"

"If it could be done without our being speared at the next Cleanup, yes. I'm afraid we're failures as rogues. This wild life doesn't suit us: I miss my food, I miss you, and I miss my proper task."

Iroedh wrinkled her nose to indicate lack of sympathy with his desires. She said:

"I have something here to show you, and a plan that may get you back on your own terms."

She unwrapped the machete and drew it from its scabbard. Antis stared wonderingly, took the implement, and, with a slowly dawning light of understanding in his eyes, hefted and swished it.

72

"Now this is something!" he cried. "Did you get this from the men?"

"Yes. They call it something like matselh." She told him the history of O'Mara and his machete. "But you may not have that!" she said.

"Why not? There's an old rogue in the Lhanwaed Hills who has learned smithery and who could duplicate this thing——"

"I have a better use for it. Did you know the Royal Duel takes place in five days?"

"No, I didn't. What about it?"

"If I offered this to Estir as a sure method of winning, don't you think she might agree to issue a pardon on her accession, and to use her influence with the Council to exempt you three permanently from the Cleanups?"

"Hmm—maybe. It's a tempting idea. But how well do you know Estir?"

"Not at all well; I've merely met her a few times at social functions. They say she has a violent temper."

"Why would you trust her?"

"A princess wouldn't lie!"

"Let's hope. I still wish I could have this thing; it makes one feel a lot less vulnerable to the whims of fortune."

"You wouldn't find it very useful for hunting. What you need are some stout bows and spears. I'll watch for a chance to steal you some."

VI. The Royal Duel

The dome of Princess Estir of Elham was heavily guarded, lest the queen, wandering in that way, make a sudden attempt at assassination. With a pass from the agricultural officer, however, Iroedh soon got her audience.

"Many eggs, Princess," she said. "Candidly, what do you think of your chances?"

Estir balanced on the balls of her feet as if sighting for a spear thrust. She was as slim and active as a worker, though her breasts were fully developed.

"I don't know," she said in a lazy voice that reminded Iroedh of the drawl of the Arsuuni. "Better than even, I should think. Of course there's always a factor of luck, but I'm in good form and my omens have been favorable."

"Maybe I could guarantee you your victory."

Estir looked sharply at Iroedh, her slit pupils widening. "You could?"

"Perhaps."

"You mean you'd want something in return, eh?"

"Right," said Iroedh.

"Say on."

"You know the three drones who disappeared?"

"Who doesn't? What about them?"

"They'd like to return to the Community."

"So? If they don't mind the little detail of being speared to death we should be glad to have them."

"But, Princess, that's just it. They want pardons and permanent exemption from the Cleanups."

"How do you know? Have you been fraternizing with them? That's a serious offense, you know."

Iroedh smiled. "Ask me no questions and I'll tell you no lies. That's what they want."

"Well?"

"If you'll see they get what they ask, I will see that you win your duel."

Estir looked puzzled. "You might almost as well ask for the Treasure of Inimdhad! That would bend our system pretty far. When you consider how many drone babies we kill to keep the population in balance, they should thank Gwyyr they've been allowed to live this long."

"It's no doubt wrong of them to wish to prolong their lives, but such is the case."

"Why should you be acting for them? A loyal worker should try to see that they're hunted down and killed."

"Princess, I won't argue the rights and wrongs of the question. If you wish to win your fight, promise the other matter. Otherwise I'll go to the queen."

Estir thought a bit. "Very well then. Show me your trick, or special prayer to Gwyyr, or whatever it is, and if I win my duel with it I promise to get your drones pardoned and exempted from future Cleanups. Do you really mean you want them allowed to live even after they're too old to perform their function?"

"Yes."

"All right. This may set a troublesome precedent, but I haven't much choice."

Iroedh unwrapped the machete and explained its use.

Estir's yellow eyes glowed. "This will do it! A dagger in the right hand for parrying spear thrusts, then get in close and slash——"

"It can also be used for thrusting," said Iroedh, "though it's a little heavy at the point for that purpose."

"It's too bad I haven't a longer time to practice, but poor old Intar will never have seen such a thing! I'll write out the pardons and postdate them to take effect the minute Intar dies. I'll also get in touch with the Council. Tell your drones to come to the duel; they shan't be molested."

"Thank you, Princess." Iroedh headed back to her cell and *A Girl of the Limberlost*.

On the day of the duel Iroedh helped all morning to carry seats out to the exercise ground. Other workers cleared away the parallel bars and other gymnastic equipment with zest, for a Royal Duel was one of their few holidays.

A guard said: "Iroedh!"

"Yes?"

"Two of the escaped drones are out at the main gate. They say they've been promised immunity, and want a document to show before they will come in."

Iroedh dropped her task to hunt up the agricultural officer, who provided her with the necessary pass. She then hurried out to the front gate, where she found Antis and Kutanas waiting, both wearing stolen workers' cloaks. She escorted them past the glowering guards, who hefted their spears significantly.

"Where's Dyos?" she asked.

Antis answered: "He didn't come; doesn't trust Estir. To tell the truth, I don't either, but I wouldn't give her the satisfaction of knowing I was afraid of her."

"How are you making out, dear?"

"Not too badly. We killed a wild leipag and had a feast."

"You look fit," she said.

"Fit if not beautiful." He laughed and slapped his belly, now nearly flat instead of the normal drone paunch. "This life certainly does things to one's shape, don't you think? I don't know if the queen will like it, whoever *is* queen tonight. I'm all excited about the duel; I wasn't yet hatched when Intar slew Queen Pligayr. What will happen if Intar should win after all?"

"This safe-conduct is good until sundown in any case."

"And then we light out for the timber again. Oh, well."

They came to the exercise ground where most of the workers of Elham had already gathered. Others were pouring in from the domes of the Community and from the fields around it. A group of workers headed by Gogledh arrived from Thidhem, having been rewarded for industry and efficiency by passes to the combat. The ushers struggled to range the crowd around the four sides of the field, a row of workers squatting on the ground in front, then one of workers seated, then one of workers standing. A picked group was performing a military dance in the open space.

"I've never seen a duel either," said Kutanas, "and I wish the dancers would stop their dancing and spear-waving and let us get on to the main event. Do they fight in armor or what?"

"No," said Iroedh. "According to the rules they must fight naked, with no shields or other defenses. The object is a quick clean victory, preferably with the victor unhurt. They may use any offensive weapons other than missile weapons. Sometimes they carry a spear in both hands, and sometimes a spear in one hand and a hatchet or dagger in the other."

The dancers finished and filed off, and a pair of workers under the direction of the grounds officer pushed a roller over the trampled sand.

An usher said: "Iroedh, these drones with you will have to sit in the drones' section—— Oh!"

"Yes, they are those that escaped, but they have a safe-conduct," said Iroedh, waving the document under the usher's nose. "As they have the status of visitors I think they should stay with me."

"Here they come," said Antis.

A murmur of the crowd presaged the appearance of Intar and Estir at opposite ends of the field, each with her seconds. Intar's efforts to train down for the fight had not been very successful. Estir, on the other hand, moved with the deadly grace of a beast of prey.

Kutanas said: "Everybody's betting on Estir, but the old queen has some tricks the other never heard of."

"You should know," said Antis.

The foreign officer (who, with the general still absent, was the senior Council member) read the traditional proclamation setting forth the reason for the duel and the qualities of the combatants. She droned on until the workers were all fidgeting.

". . . so, for the good of Elham, you will enter upon this

sacred fray resolved to prosecute it to the death, and may the best queen win! Begin!"

Intar lumbered down from her end, her rolls of fat jouncing, while Estir trotted lightly from hers. The queen carried a standard guard's spear in both hands; the princess a dagger in one hand and O'Mara's machete in the other. The crowd muttered its surprise at the sight of the latter weapon. Iroedh caught phrases:

"What's that thing?" ". . . unfair; the Council shouldn't allow . . ." "Why don't we use those in war?" "I wish to withdraw my bet on Intar!"

"Iroedh darling!" said Vardh. "I feel just sure Intar will win. Remember the Oracle of Ledhwid:

> *"When the female ueg with curving claw*
> *Shall lop the head of a pomual bloom,*
> *She shall stand on her head on a vremoel raw*
> *Or fall to her doom."*

"You applied that same stanza to the plague last year," Iroedh reminded her.

The queen braced herself, hands wide apart on the spear shaft, and thrust at Estir as the princess came on. Estir threw herself to one side with lightning quickness and swung the machete. Intar parried with the spearhead; there was a clang of metal.

The females circled warily, now and then making a short rush or feint. Queen Intar thrust with her point, then quickly reversed the spear and swung the butt end at Estir's ankles in an effort to trip her. Estir leaped over the shaft and made a downward cut at Intar's head. Intar whipped up the spear shaft and the machete blade bit into the wood.

"I think," said Antis, "Estir's going slowly, to tire out Intar before closing."

The fighters were circling again, with long periods of feinting and footwork at a distance and then an occasional quick flurry of blows and thrusts.

"Ah-h!" went the crowd.

Estir had not been quick enough in recovering after delivering a cut, and the spearhead jabbed her shoulder. As it was the right, the one that held the dagger, she seemed none the worse, though blood trickled down in a red rill and fell in slow drops from her fingers.

Advance, retreat, feint, parry, thrust, recover. On and on they went. Intar suddenly rushed in and thrust with surprising agility. Estir parried with the machete and thrust out with her dagger. The point pricked Intar's sagging left breast. Blood trickled there too.

Vardh said to Iroedh: "Darling, I'm so sure Intar's going to win I've bet my year's clothing allowance on her. I've been saying a special prayer to Eunmar; did you know I believe in the old gods? If you try hard enough, I've found, you can believe anything."

After another pause Intar pressed the fight again, driving Estir before her with quick jabs. As the princess parried one at her face with the dagger, Intar jerked the pike back and thrust again, low. The point struck Estir in the thigh—not squarely, but glancing, opening another small wound.

As Intar withdrew the spear for another thrust, Estir dropped her dagger and caught the spear shaft just back of the head. She pulled it toward herself and struck with the machete at the queen's right hand. The blade bit into the hand.

With a yell the queen released her hold on the shaft with that hand. She stepped back, blood spraying the sand, and tugged at the shaft with her good hand. Estir resisted for a second, then pushed. Intar stumbled backward and sat down.

Estir, leaping forward, brought the machete down in a full overhand slash. The blade sank deep into Intar's left shoulder. Her left arm went limp and Estir tore the spear out of her grasp and threw it away.

Intar took a last look at the opponent towering over her, then closed her eyes and bowed her head. The machete whistled through the air and sheared through the queen's thick neck. Spouting blood, the body collapsed and lay kicking and twitching.

Estir walked toward the table where the foreign officer sat, kicked the dead queen's head aside as she went, and cried: "I, Estir of Elham, being a fertile and functional female of pure Elhamny descent, and having slain my predecessor Intar in fair fight in accordance with the laws and customs of Elham, do hereby proclaim myself Queen of Elham!"

The foreign officer cried: "Homage to the new Queen of Elham!"

All the workers and drones dropped to their knees, shouting: "Hail to the queen! *Kwa Estir!* Long life and many eggs!"

Vardh said to Iroedh: "Isn't she just the most beautiful thing, like one of the prophecies come to life? I can forgive her for making me lose my bets."

78

Iroedh had to admit that, even with blood still trickling down her skin from her wounds, Estir made a magnificent picture. It was too bad, she thought, that there were no artists nowadays like those of yore who could do justice to the scene.

Vardh continued: "Let's try to arrange to be in her escort to the next Queens' Conference, darling. The round dances will be ever such fun."

Before Iroedh could answer (the noise having somewhat abated) Estir cried: "As the first act of my reign, I revoke the safe-conduct pass given to the rogue drones Antis and Kutanas. Slay them, guards, and arrest the worker Iroedh for treason!"

Iroedh looked blankly at the new queen, at the foreign officer, and at her drones, who looked equally thunderstruck. She shouted back:

"But, Queen, you promised——"

"I promised nothing! Guards, obey my commands!"

Even as the guards poised their spears and started toward them, Antis and Kutanas moved. Out from under their cloaks came two more machetes—near copies of the one wielded by Estir, but red-brown bronze instead of gray steel, and more crudely made.

"Stand back!" roared Antis, swinging his machete.

The unarmed workers scattered. Antis pulled a third machete from the belt he wore under his cloak and thrust the hilt at Iroedh.

"Take it!" he said.

"But——"

"*Take it!*"

Though unaccustomed to being ordered around by a drone, Iroedh took the machete just in time to knock aside the point of a spear.

"Make for the main gate!" said Antis, swinging wildly.

One of his blows knocked the helmet from the head of a guard; another cut through the shaft of a spear; another laid open a guard's arm and sent her back, bleeding. Kutanas was likewise busy; a guard went down under his blows with her guts spilling onto the sand.

Iroedh took a few swipes and heard her blade clank against the brass of the guards' defenses. Then all at once the way lay open before the fugitives. Antis seized Iroedh's free hand with his and ran for the gate, right through the flower beds. Behind them they could hear the screams of Queen Estir above the general uproar.

"Open up!" bellowed Antis as they neared the gate. "Emergency!"

Whatever the guards at the gate thought, they stood staring in silent incomprehension as the fugitives threw back the bolt and pushed open the gate. Then one of them said:

"Come back here! There's something irregular about this. Why are those people chasing you?"

"Ask them!" said Antis and dragged Iroedh out.

They ran toward the field of tarhail into which Iroedh had dropped the drones from the helicopter. Behind them came the sound of the pursuit, slowed by the fact that none of the unarmed workers seemed anxious to run on ahead of the guards, while the guards, weighted down with shields and cuirasses, could not run so fast as an unencumbered Avtin.

They panted across the field and into the woods on the far side. Now, thought Iroedh, the agricultural officer would have another trampled swath to fume about; it was a shame to do such a thing to her best friend on the Council. But since through force of circumstances she was becoming a hardened anti-Communitarian, she did not give the matter much thought.

Antis led her this way and that along trails through the woods.

"Old game trails," he said. "We can rest now. It'll take them hours to find us in this maze."

When Iroedh got her breath she asked: "Where's Kutanas?"

"Dead. Didn't you see the guards get him?"

"No. I was too busy fighting on my own account."

"He looked like a spiny dhug by the time they finished shoving their spears into him. Too bad, because he'd have made a better rogue than that fat fool Dyos, who is always complaining and afraid of his own shadow."

"And the fat fool lives, while the worthy Kutanas lies dead. *Weu!* I feel terrible about having fought my fellow workers. Maybe I even slew one. And to have Estir act in that treacherous manner! If one cannot trust one's own queen, whom can one trust?"

"Oneself. Cheer up; such is life."

"Where did you get the matselhi?"

"That old smith I told you about, Umwys, made them from my description. We hauled that statue of Dhiis playing a telh that we found in Khinam all the way to his hideout to supply the metal."

"You didn't!" cried Iroedh.

"Of course we did! What of it?"

"But that's a priceless relic——"

80

"Maybe it is, but without that bronze we should all be dead. Since we had nothing to pay Umwys with, we had to give him the bronze left over from the making of the matselhi. He's been working day and night on those things ever since I saw you at Khinam. Are you rested enough to go on?"

"I think so."

"Let's go to our rendezvous with Dyos, then."

He led her on and on until Iroedh was completely lost, for as she had not had hunting duty for several years, she no longer knew the woods beyond the Community's fields and pastures very well. At last he came to a little hilltop.

"*Prutha!*" he cried. "The rascal's run away and taken with him that bow-and-arrow set I was making!"

"What luck! What shall we do, then?"

"Go on to Umwys's hide-out, I suppose. If he has some spare food we may get a supper of sorts."

He led the way again. The going became more and more rugged as they climbed into the Lhanwaed Hills. Iroedh was staggering with fatigue when Antis put his hands to his mouth and gave a peculiar call. When it was answered he led Iroedh to a place where the brush was almost impassable.

Antis pushed a mass of vegetation aside and ducked into a hole that led right into the hillside. The tunnel did a sharp turn, and Iroedh found herself able to stand upright again in an illuminated chamber hollowed out of the hill. Wooden props supported a ceiling of hewn boards. Other openings led in other directions.

A wrinkled old drone faced them. When he saw Iroedh he gave a gasp, whipped up a spear he was holding, and hurled it right at her.

The point was headed straight for her midriff when Antis knocked it up with his machete. The spear stuck quivering in the ceiling.

"What's the matter, you old fool?" roared Antis.

"I thought you'd betrayed me to the workers," said Umwys in his whining northern accent. "Every worker's hand is against me, and mine is against every worker."

"Iroedh is no longer a worker, but a rogue like you and me. Now apologize for trying to kill her!"

"I never heard of a rogue worker," said Umwys sullenly. "But if he says you are, I suppose you are. It'll be your fault, Antis, if she brings the whole Community of Elham down upon our necks. What d'you want with me, eh? To buy somewhat more of weapons?"

"No. I want to know what's become of Dyos. He failed to meet us as promised, and I think he's run off."

"He may have at that. He was asking about the rogue bands to the north."

"Then we're stuck again. Can you put us up for the night?"

"You may sleep here, and I can furnish you with a little meat. If she wants a meal she'll have to get her own, for I have no worker fodder. There be some khal trees with edible seeds on the hillside."

Iroedh slipped out to forage; an unrewarding job, taking till sundown to collect enough nuts to half fill her stomach. Umwys, however, had lost some of his hostility in the meantime.

"You don't seem like a worker, lass," he said. "Why, you're nice!"

Not knowing quite how to take this, Iroedh munched her seeds in silence.

"If I were in your fix," said Umwys, sucking marrow, "I'd head north to Ledhwid and ask the Oracle for advice."

"What?" said Iroedh. "You sound like my mystical friend Vardh. All the responses from Ledhwid I ever heard could be taken in any of sixteen different ways."

"No, aside from those daft verses, the Oracle sometimes offers canny advice. Nothing mystical, just logical inferences from the news its priestesses bring it. At least that's the best course I can think of. You can't live off this land; there's not enough game or wild vegetable food, and if you raid the Communities, with but the two of ye against hundreds of them, they'll hunt you down."

Antis asked: "Why shouldn't we join one of the rogue bands to the north?"

"You could, but they'd slay her on sight. The rogues' attitude toward workers is to strike first and inquire afterwards."

"That seems unreasonable," said Iroedh.

"Eh, yes, but they feel they've been used unreasonably too. Now the band of Wythias is growing so great it could even attack a fortified Community, the way the Arsuuni do. I have enough orders from Wythias for spearheads to keep me busy half a year."

Iroedh asked: "If the rogue bands help the Arsuuni to destroy all the Avtiny Communities, what would then become of the drones? The whole race would perish."

"You'd better ask Wythias about that; or, better yet, the Oracle, for Wythias wouldn't let you live long enough to get the question out. If the Oracle can't think of anything better for you to do, you might be able to take service with it."

"With the Oracle?" said Iroedh.

"Aye. It employs somewhat of—ah—orphaned workers like yourself."

"I know. I've seen the so-called priestesses. But what would happen to Antis?"

"How should I know? I don't think the Oracle employs drones, so he might have to join a rogue band after all."

"We won't be separated!" said Antis.

Umwys shrugged. "It's your lives, billies. Maybe he could leave his band to come see you once an eight-day, eh? Though where you two get that unnatural attachment for each other I can't think."

"Ledhwid shall it be then," said Antis.

"You'll need a cloak for her," said Umwys. "If you have to sleep in the open she'll get somewhat cold without clothing. And you'd better collect some vegetable food for her. Several of the plants have edible roots and berries and things, but having nought to do with workers I don't know which is which."

Next day Antis said: "We'll get you a cloak the same way I got mine. Come along."

They hiked back toward Elham. After some hours Antis motioned for caution as they neared the cultivated fields.

"Down there," he whispered.

"Down there" a small group of workers was mowing a field of tarhail—the very field, in fact, they had fled through the previous afternoon. Evidently the agricultural officer was determined not to wait for any more of her crop to be trampled.

At one side of the field a worker stood guard over the cloaks, food, water, and other gear. The guard was armed with spear, shield, and helmet, but no body armor, as this was normally not a hazardous job.

"What do we do now?" said Iroedh.

"Wait."

"How long?"

"All day if need be. You have no idea of the patience required to be a successful thief."

And wait for hours they did, lying on their bellies under the shrubs at the crest of the hill. At long last the guard yawned and sat down with her back to a tree.

Antis grinned. "It's the boredom that gets them. Now watch."

83

For another hour they watched. The guard chewed a grass stem, yawned some more, and turned over a stone to look at the creeping things under it.

"There she goes," said Antis.

The guard slid down further and pulled the helmet over her face. From where Iroedh lay the guard looked like some bifurcated pink vegetable with a nutshell covering one end.

Antis rose to a crouch, beckoned, and stole down the game trail to the border of the field. On the way he picked up a dead branch as long as himself. This he maneuvered with exquisite care among the trees. When they got to where Iroedh could again see the red of the guard's skin through the green of the foliage, Antis held up a hand to halt her. He slid behind a big tree and reached around it with the stick, holding it out like a spear at full lunge. Gently he poked the point of the stick under the collar of one of the cloaks.

The guard stirred and muttered in her sleep.

Antis froze, then moved again. He raised the cloak off the branch stub that served as a peg, then drew back branch and cloak. He leaned the branch against his big tree, rolled up the cloak, and flashed a grin at Iroedh.

Iroedh glanced around to pick the route of retreat, and, as she did so, something caught her eye. Something bulky hanging from a tree.

With a vaguely reassuring motion to Antis she stepped lightly around the intervening trunks. The object proved to be a big bag, hanging like the cloaks from the stub of a branch. She lifted it down. Inside was a mass of biscuit flour and a sheet of vakhwil bark with writing on it.

She stalked back to where she had left Antis, holding the bag, and together they stole away from the clearing. When they were safely over the hill he said:

"What's that?"

Iroedh dug in and brought out the sheet. On it was a note reading:

From one who stays behind to one who has gone away:

Here, dearest, is something that may come in handy in the strenuous days to come, as you will have trouble finding proper nourishment among the meat-eating rogues. Think kindly of one who loves and admires you. I still think you would have made a wonderful foreign officer. And whether the old gods exist or not, I pray to them to watch over you. If you get downhearted, remember what the Oracle of Ledhwid said about the two-headed queen riding the blue vakhnag.

"Vardh!" said Iroedh. "The dear child!"

Though the note was unsigned she had no difficulty guessing the identity of the sender. Her throat closed up and she gave a slight sob.

Antis said: "There's no luck like a true friend, as the Oracle once said. Now we're fixed for the journey."

Hand in hand they started off for the cave of Umwys, Gliid, and Ledhwid, with Iroedh whistling the *Song of Geyliad*.

VII. *The Rogue Drones*

As they neared the *Paris*, five days later, Antis showed increasing signs of unease.

"Are you sure?" he said, "these creatures won't eat us, or the sky ship won't fall over and crush us? It looks very unstable."

"Quite sure," said Iroedh. "What's the matter with my hero, my second Idhios, who has so lightly eluded the search parties from Elham, and who has driven off a prowling noag with a piece of firewood? Has your courage all oozed away?"

"Avtiny workers and noags I know about," he retorted in a sharp tone, "but only fools rush into unknown dangers."

While he spoke, Iroedh had been preparing a second and sharper gibe, but withheld it rather than foment a quarrel. Certainly he had shown enough courage and force of character during their perilous journey afoot to Gliid for three normal drones. In fact, she found herself depending upon him instead of the other way round, as an Avtin would normally expect.

Presently they came upon the clearing around the *Paris*. Iroedh was surprised to see a row of chariots parked in the place where Rhodh's party had camped, and a herd of uegs of about equal numbers tethered nearby. A man was feeding the beasts.

Iroedh, followed by a hesitant Antis, went up to the man and asked in English: "Where is Dr. Bloch to be found, please?" As her lisping Avtiny accent made the sentence into "Hwerydh Daktablak tubi thaund, pliidh?" it took her some time to make herself clear.

"Over there, on the other side of the ship," said the man.

They continued on until they found Bloch, with Barbe Dulac and another man, working on the ground beyond the ship. The Terrans had spread a dead leipag out on the ground and taken the beast thoroughly apart. The hide had already come off and was stretched out, with the inside up, while the other man did mysterious things to it. Meanwhile Bloch was removing all the muscles and organs from the skeleton, which had by now been nearly freed of them. Every few seconds he stopped to dictate notes to Barbe, or to tell her to draw a sketch or point a camera at the remains, or he would pop an organ into a jar full of some colorless but strong-smelling liquid. The male men were covered with blood and stank.

After Iroedh had watched for a while, Bloch looked up and said: "Hello. It is—it's Iroedh of Elham, is it not?"

"Certainly," said Iroedh, a little surprised that he should have trouble remembering her. "This is Antis, also of Elham."

"Excuse my not shaking hands," said Bloch, twiddling his gory fingers. "But——"

"What does he mean?" said Antis.

"Our form of greeting," continued Bloch, his Avtinyk more fluent than on the previous visit. "And what is a drone doing so far from his dronery? Oh, I know! You're one of the drones we hoisted out of the prison cell! What happened after that?"

"I owe you more than thanks," said Antis with dignity. "Any time I can do you a good turn, speak up."

When Iroedh had finished her story she said: "And so we are bound for Ledhwid and the Oracle. Have you thought of going there? I'm sure it would interest you."

"Now that," said Bloch, "is a remarkable—how would you say 'coincidence'? For only yesterday a worker named Yaedh of Yeym arrived here, saying she came from this Oracle and inviting us to call."

Iroedh said: "She'd be one of the Oracle's priestesses. Yeym was destroyed by the Arsuuni, and she would also be one of the few left alive from that Community. Do you plan to go?"

"Yes. We haven't obtained access to a single Community yet, and we cannot remain here much longer——"

"Why not? Where are you going?"

"The *Paris* is going to sample every continent on your planet, which means ten or twelve stops. As I was saying, Barbe would like a—how would you say 'honeymoon trip'?"

After some explanation, Iroedh said: "Oh, you're now her official drone! I should like to ask some questions about that——"

"Not just now, please," said Bloch. "So, since she's accustomed to roughing it also, we thought that would make an agreeable one. The only difficulty is we cannot spare enough men from the *Paris* to make up a party of safe size. Hence your coming is very convenient, and I suppose you would rather ride than walk, wouldn't you?"

"Certainly," said Iroedh. "Is this Yaedh of Yeym here at Gliid, and is she coming with us?"

"Yes. She's around somewhere."

"Have any other Avtini visited your sky ship since our departure?"

"Several. A delegation arrived from Khwiem to request us to arbitrate some dispute with a neighboring Community. We had to turn them down——"

"Turn them down? You mean throw them down? Why——"

"No; I meant refuse their request. A couple of others put in an appearance just to see what they could observe. And then a great tall creature, one of the Arshuul—you call them Arsuuni, don't you?—came with a warning from Queen Omförs of Tvaar (which I take it is your Omvyr of Tvaarm) that if we dared to interfere in their program of conquest they would fill us full of spears."

Bloch seemed amused by this threat, which fact puzzled Iroedh (who had a healthy fear of the Arsuuni) until she remembered the awesome powers of the men. If she could only somehow arrange for the Arsuuni to attack the Terran expedition . . .

She asked: "How are you going to Ledhwid?"

"The same way you travel—in ueg chariots. Didn't you see those we have bought from Thidhem?"

"Why should you go that way when you can fly there in a few hours?"

"Two reasons: We don't know if there is a proper landing place for the helicopter at Ledhwid, and we can see much more of the planet by crawling around on its surface than by flying over it. Moreover, if we go in the chariots we can get acquainted with the people, whereas if they see us flying they're likely to run for cover and stay hidden until we've gone. We've been through all this on other planets."

"What if you get into some serious danger or difficulty?"

"We shall keep in communication with the *Paris* so that if necessary Kang can fly out and rescue us."

Iroedh asked: "How can you talk with the ship when you're sixteens of borbi away?"

Bloch smiled. "Terran magic. By the way, do you know who or what the Oracle is? Yaedh won't tell."

"No. It's a living creature, but aside from that I don't know if it's queen, worker, or drone; or even whether it's Avtin or Arsuun. It never meets its clients face to face. When do we start?"

"Tomorrow morning, now that you're here. Can Antis drive one of these things?"

Iroedh exchanged looks with Antis, who said: "I'm not really good, since drones aren't normally expected to learn that art, but Iroedh has taught me enough to manage. If you don't fear the results, I don't."

Next morning they hitched up five of the uegs before sunrise.

Yaedh of Yeym had shown up the previous evening with a bagful of fungi of kinds that the uegs particularly liked, and which she had been out gathering when Iroedh arrived. As a result of Yaedh's pampering the beasts adored her and obeyed her every command. She was a lean and elderly worker with wrinkles on her face and her crest faded from scarlet to pale pink, who said but little.

The road ran down the floor of the valley toward the outlet, winding among the great boulders scattered around the defile at the northern or lower end. The day was uneventful. They stopped and set up camp toward sunset. Bloch took a thing like a little flat box out of his pocket, twisted some knobs, and spoke into it.

Iroedh asked: "What on Niond are you doing, Dakta-blak?"

"Reporting to the *Paris*."

"You can actually talk to the sky ship with that little thing?"

"Certainly. Would you care to say hello to Subbarau?"

Iroedh looked doubtfully at the little box. "Hail, Captain Subbarau," she said in a weak voice.

"How are you, Madame Iroedh?" came back Subbarau's nasal tones.

Iroedh hastily handed the box back to Bloch. After they had eaten and Bloch was puffing on his pipe and Antis practicing with his telh, Iroedh said to Barbe:

"Bardylak dear, I should like to ask some questions about you and Daktablak. First——"

"Hey!" said Bloch when he heard the first question. "That's a Kinsey."

"What's a kyndhi?"

"A type of interrogation named for a man who invented it long ago. You can't ask just anybody that; it's against our customs."

"Then how do you learn what you must know in order to——"

"You may ask me the questions in private."

Barbe spoke up: "Not to change the subject or anything, but what became of that book I gave you, Iroedh?"

"I read more than halfway through before I had to flee. That's one reason I wish to get back into the Community."

"How far did you get?"

"To where the two females, Elnora and Edith, each wants the drone Philip to fertilize her. At least I think that's what it means, though it's hard to be sure, because in matters of propagation Terrans never say anything right out, but use subtle hints."

"I can tell you——" began Barbe, but Iroedh cut her off:

"Oh, please don't! I still hope to recover the book some day."

Bloch asked; "What book is this?" and when told, exploded: "My God! With Tolstoy and Lewis and Balzac, and Conrad and Silberstein and Hemingway and McNaughton and a hundred other *good* novelists to choose from, you introduce her to the glories of Terran literature with one of the worst pieces of sentimental slush ever written!"

"It is not!" said Barbe. "It's just that you're such an introvert, you, that you don't appreciate how other human beings——"

"What is 'slush'?" said Iroedh.

Nobody heeded her. Barbe, getting excited, switched to French, which left Iroedh completely at a loss, especially since Bloch replied in the same language. The men waved their arms and blabbered at a furious rate, and ended up

89

apologizing and hugging each other and making that curious mouth-touching gesture. They returned to English, in which Iroedh caught frequent use of the word "love."

"This love of yours," she said, "seems to play a large part in Barbe's book. From all I gather, love of individuals is more important among you than love of your Community. If that's the case, how can your Communities be well run?"

"Mostly they aren't," said Bloch, relighting his pipe. "But we have a lot of fun."

"Oh, come now," said Barbe, "we love our Communities too. Besides Winston I also love my home city of Genève, me, and my country of Helvetia . . ."

"That's not the same sort of thing," said Bloch. "It's a matter of the language. Barbe's language has only one word, *aimer,* to represent all grades of affection. In English we confine 'love' to the more profound emotion, like that which Barbe and I feel for each other, and use 'like' for the milder and more superficial——"

Barbe interrupted: "Now don't tell me you only *like* your country and your home region! I have heard your rhapsodies on the United States of America and on Bucks County, Pennsylvania, in particular——"

"Oh, all right, I suppose I do," said Bloch, puffing. "What we really require, I suppose, is about six words to represent all grades of love. At the top we should put love for one's mate, then love for one's parents and children, then for other close friends and relatives, then for one's locale and one's work, and so on."

Barbe said: "Do not claim you merely *like* your work either, Winston darling! I often think you love it better than me——"

"Not the same sort of thing at all," said Bloch. "Iroedh, I suppose that with you the Community comes at the top?"

"Normally, yes."

Bloch said: "We once had a sect or cult on Terra called Communists, who believed as you do that love of the Community should take precedence over all others. But their collectivistic love seemed to involve such fanatical hatred of everybody else and such implacable determination to impose their system on the world that we had to exterminate them. However, I suppose you are a somewhat special case because of your estrangement from your Community."

"Yes," said Iroedh. "I'm so confused I don't know if I love my Community or Antis the better."

Antis spoke up: "I have no doubts at all; I love Iroedh the best of anything, and say a plague upon the Community! Since leaving it I've been a real person instead of a mere stud animal."

"Thank you, Antis," said Iroedh. "Of course I don't think we could ever have a love in the strongest sense in which the men use the term, because that seems to be connected with sex."

"And it is impossible for you, that there?" said Barbe.

"Certainly. I'm a neuter. But even if I never go back to Elham, I shall manage, so long as I can love Antis and perhaps my antiquities."

Bloch said: "You must love your antiques in the same way I love my work." He asked Antis: "Did you never feel this most violent grade of love for the queen when you—ah——"

"When I tupped her? By Eunmar, that was just work! Though I won't say I disliked old Intar, who was not a bad sort. When she——" The drone stopped. "Anyhow, it is perhaps just as well that the question of sex cannot arise between Iroedh and myself. The more I hear of you men, the more I think our love will be better without that element."

"That's what *you* think," said Barbe. "Me, I can tell you a different story; but since you are of another species it would not mean anything to you." She turned to Yaedh. "You have said nothing, sister. What or whom do you love, and why?"

Yaedh drew patterns in the dirt. "Like any normal worker, I loved my Community," she said, throwing a severe glance toward Iroedh. "When that was destroyed I had nothing left. Nothing. All I can love now is animals; that's why I feed delicacies to the uegs and keep a neinog at Ledhwid."

"How about your fellow priestesses?" asked Iroedh.

Yaedh shrugged. "They are from many Communities, but do not themselves constitute a Community. While I like most of them well enough, there is no comparison with one's feeling for one's own Community. It's the difference between those Terran words 'like' and 'love' Daktablak was telling us about."

Bloch said: "How about the Oracle himself—or herself? Does he, she, or it inspire love?"

"We are not allowed to discuss the Oracle. I can however tell you that it is neither male nor female in the sense we know." After a pause she resumed: "My only advice to all of you would be to love as much and as many things and people as possible, so you shan't be so empty-hearted when you lose one of them. *My* only comfort is the oracular quatrain that goes:

> *"When the last sun sets and the stars grow cold*
> *And the one-eyed queen has laid her last,*
> *Then a new birth shall on Niond unfold*
>   *When the old has passed."*

"Cold comfort," said Bloch. "Like most oracular verse, full of vague ominous intimations of nothing in particular. But who am I to spoil your one pleasure?"

When Iroedh and Antis had gone to bed on the air mattresses provided by the *Viagens Interplanetarias,* wrapped in their cloaks and each other's arms for warmth, Bloch came and stood over them.

"Well," he said, "perhaps you overgrown children are physically unable to experience our kind of love, but you seem to do all right."

For three days the journey northward progressed with little event except an occasional rain. Iroedh, feeling herself no longer bound by her Community's commands, passed on to Bloch her considerable knowledge of Avtiny history and culture. Barbe listened attentively, taking it all down in shorthand.

Bloch said: "I should like to inspect that ruined city of Khinam. Do you suppose the Elhamni would try to chase us off if we paid it a visit before we left?"

"They know about your guns," said Iroedh. "They might not like it, but I don't think they would try anything drastic."

"Then we will try to work in a visit—— Hello, what's this ahead?"

"This" was a waist-high pile of logs and rocks across the road. Iroedh's eye caught a flash of brass.

"Rogues!" she cried. "Get your gun ready, Daktablak!"

Bloch cried *"Branio!"* to his ueg, which obediently halted. He looked around nervously while unslinging the gun from his shoulder, saying:

"Do you think—uh—perhaps we could get the chariots turned around and run for it?"

"Too late," said Antis, whipping out his bronze machete. "Look back there!"

A group of Avtiny drones had debouched on to the road behind them and were running toward them, all but one of them, who paused to aim a bow. There were two or three shields and helmets in the group, and one cuirass, but otherwise they were naked and carried only spears and the one bow.

Antis grinned at Iroedh, swishing his blade through the air. "If Daktablak could kill those with the armor, we could take it from them——"

Yaedh of Yeym called loudly: "Priestess of the Oracle of Ledhwid! I claim immun——"

Whssht! went the arrow released by the archer. Yaedh and Antis cut off their speeches to duck.

"Up ahead!" exclaimed Yaedh.

A similar group of irregulars had come around the road block in front.

"Get back here, Antis!" said Iroedh, drawing her own blade. "Let's keep together and let the men deal with them at a distance. Then if they get close——"

Crack! Iroedh's eardrums shook painfully to the discharge of Barbe's pistol. The little female man had run to the tail of the column and fired past Yaedh's chariot. The leading drone among the attackers spun around and fell in the roadway.

Barbe screamed: "You shoot those in front, while I——"

Tactactactac! went Bloch's gun, echoed by another crack of the pistol. Then both weapons crashed together. One of the uegs upset its chariot in its terror. The racket made Iroedh wince and shut her eyes. Though she was a qualified soldier of her Community, this was as unnerving as her first helicopter flight had been.

Tactactac! Crack!

When Iroedh opened her eyes, the rogues to the rear were scattering to the shelter of the woods, leaving two of their number lying in the road. In front they were likewise running away or scrambling over the barrier. Three lay sprawled in that direction. The last to climb the barricade paused at the top to look back. Bloch raised the gun and with a single shot sent the drone flying into the road beyond.

The frightened uegs had tried to bolt, but Yaedh was calming them down by talking to them. Iroedh shook her head to get the ringing out of her ears.

"A short fight," said Antis. "I never got a chance to show what I could do."

"The fiends!" said Yaedh. "I can understand their attacking the rest of you, but to assault a priestess of the Oracle is unheard-of. This must be the band of Wythias; he's the only rogue leader ruthless enough to commit such an atrocity."

"Are you hurt, darling?" said Barbe to her husband.

"N-no, just a little shaken," said Bloch, doing things with his gun. Sweat stood out on his face as though he had been running. "This must be what happened to the party from the Osirian ship."

"Great Eunmar!" said Antis, who had walked over to look at a dead drone. "The magic weapon certainly smashes them up. This one has hardly any head left!"

Bloch said: "Let's right this chariot and clear the junk out of the road."

"As soon as I collect some armor," said Antis, tugging at the chin strap of the helmet on one of the corpses. "Help me, Iroedh." He got the helmet off and wiggled his own head into it. "A little loose, but with extra padding it'll do. It's a good piece; I recognize the work of Umwys. It's too bad Bardylak made a hole in this breastplate, but I can hammer the points back in place with a stone and later have a smith patch it."

Iroedh said: "Why bother with those heavy things when the Terran weapons go right through them as if they were vakhwil bark?"

"We may not always have Terrans on our side. Try this helmet. Now, don't I look like a proper warrior out of the old epics?"

Antis stood up proudly in his cuirass and buckler and helmet and leaned on one of the dead drones' spears. Iroedh thought he certainly did look impressive. Barbe, however, made an odd sniffing noise and covered her mouth with her hands.

"Yes?" said Antis.

Barbe said: "Me, I got some fluff up my nose. You look magnificent, Antis; but shouldn't it cover—I mean, should there not be one of those things to protect you below the cuirass?"

"A military kilt?" said Antis gravely. "So there should be, except that none of our late enemies was wearing one. I shall get one eventually."

He turned to help Bloch right the upset chariot and remove the barricade. Iroedh was astonished at the ease with which he picked up logs and hurled them into the brush.

"How strong you've become!" she said.

"The simple life." Grinning, Antis heaved a stone that Iroedh thought no two workers could have lifted, jerked it to chest height with his great arm muscles standing out, and tossed it into the woods.

"Don't show off or you'll injure yourself," said Bloch.

Antis turned and appeared about to launch a tart reply when there was another *whssht!* and an arrow streaked by inches from Barbe's face.

"They're attacking again!" she cried, jerking out her pistol. "Iroedh, did you see where that came from?"

Barbe pointed the pistol this way and that at the silent forest.

"No, I didn't," said Iroedh. "Daktablak, come back here and cover us with your gun. I'll help Antis."

"But—that's not female work," blithered Bloch.

"Do as she says!" said Barbe. "She has better sense than you!"

"Oh, all right—all right." Bloch, looking harassed, climbed back on to his chariot and began sweeping the woods with his gun sights, first one side and then the other. Iroedh grunted and strained over the last logs.

Whssht! went another arrow, and struck Bloch full in the chest with a loud thump.

Bloch staggered, almost fell out of his chariot, and fired a burst into the section of woods from which the arrow had come. Antis and Iroedh had just carried the last log off the road and dropped it. They turned at the sound of a high scream from Barbe. The female man fired her pistol several times at random toward the woods, then leaped up to seize Bloch.

Iroedh ran back. Bloch stood upright in his vehicle and seemed to be wrestling with Barbe, though the arrow still protruded from his chest.

"No, no, I'm all right I tell you!" he protested. "Get back in your buggy and let's get the hell out of here!"

"Aren't you dead? Aren't you hurt?" said Barbe.

"Not a scratch! Shall we go on or back? I'm for turning back——"

"When we're three quarters of the way there?" said Barbe. "You are getting soft in the head, my old. Of course we shall go on!"

"Well, let's go either way, only quickly! You two, get aboard!"

Iroedh and Antis leaped into their chariots and cracked their whips. The uegs, impatient from the wait and nervous from the shooting, raced away with long strides, the chariots bouncing and bumping behind, and lurching to dangerous angles as they rolled over the corpses, which nobody had thought to remove from the road. Iroedh thought she heard shouts from the woods around the road block, but if so the shouters were soon left.

Yaedh called up from the rear of the line: "You had

95

better make good time, because that Wythias is a very persistent fellow. He may follow us."

"How about you?" said Iroedh to Bloch. "Are men invulnerable, or have you armor under your tunic?"

Bloch wrenched out the arrow and threw it away. "Hit my damned radio. If it's broken, as I expect, the results may be almost as serious ... I didn't know you Avtini went in for archery."

"Ordinarily we use it only for hunting," said Iroedh, "because arrows won't pierce armor. Seeing us unarmored, the drones thought to use their hunting bows on us."

Barbe said: "I'm sure a strong Terran bow could penetrate this thin brass, at least at close range."

"Maybe they haven't the right kind of wood," said Bloch, "at least on this continent."

Iroedh went into a daydream wherein she arranged with the Community of Khwiem, which specialized in marine trade, to get a cargo of some superior bow wood from another continent for the benefit of Elham.

Then she remembered that the Arsuuny war would be over long before she could effect any such transaction, and that, furthermore, she was now an outcast from Elham—an "orphan" like Yaedh. The thought of having no Community made her feel woebegone. Of course she had Antis, but one couldn't dedicate oneself to a single drone, however admirable, with the wholehearted devotion one gave a Community. If one were a Terran one could choose a mate of the opposite sex and apply one's *oedhurh* to this person, but as a neuter she was denied even this outlet ...

They passed the junction of the road to Khwiem and the distant smoking cone of Mount Wisgad. The sky had clouded over and the uegs were puffing and staggering when they drew up, well after sunset. Bloch insisted on camping well off the road, so they plowed around in the brush and trees until they found an open space on the side of a stony hill whence they had a good view of their surroundings but could not be easily seen from the road.

Bloch pulled the radio out of his breast pocket, opened it up, looked it over by the light of another Terran device (a little cylinder with a light in its end) and threw it away.

"Hopeless," he said. "It will be all right, though, because when they don't receive my report this evening Subbarau will send Kang out to search for us. He can't overlook us on that road. Hey, Antis! Belay the music!"

For Antis had just played a run on his flute. Bloch turned to Yaedh. "Don't you think we are far enough in advance of them to be safe?"

"I am not sure," said Yaedh. "There is a short cut over Mount Wisgad which, if they marched all night, might bring them up to us by morning."

"Then we'll depart before morning. How much farther to Ledhwid?"

"If we leave early and drive hard we should reach it by tomorrow's nightfall."

"Would this tough character Wythias go so far as to attack the Oracle itself?"

Yaedh hesitated. "Had you asked me that yesterday I should have said the idea was absurd. All folk hold the Oracle in reverence, or at least respect it for its practical benefits. Workers of all Communities, even those at war with one another, meet freely and peacefully there, even Arsuuni. They exchange news and negotiate treaties. Now, however, that Wythias (if it indeed be he) has failed to respect my immunity, I am not sure what he will do."

Bloch said: "In any case, we'll set up a double watch." He was fastening a tubular thing to his gun. "Barbe and I will take turns with the rifle and with one of you Avtini."

Iroedh asked: "What's that thing on your *gon?*"

"It enables us to see as well at night as one of you. Now help me arrange our gear in a circle, and then we'll turn in."

Iroedh had one of the later watches with Barbe, who said: "Your nights are all so dark here! I don't think I should care to live on Ormazd, without a moon."

It was dark, even Iroedh admitted, though never having seen a moon she could not compare her own world's nights with those of another. There was no sound except the regular snores of Winston Bloch and the chirp and buzz of nocturnal creeping things.

Then Iroedh stopped pacing and froze, moving her head this way and that to let her little round ears pick up the faintest sound. She could have sworn by Gwyyr that she had heard the faint noise of metal striking metal.

"Iroedh?" said Barbe. "What is it?"

"Quiet. Somebody's coming."

"Let's wake the others——" began Barbe, but then a voice cried:

"Kwa, Wythias!"

And the cry was taken up all around: "Kwa, Wythias! Kwa, Wythias!" Heavy bodies moved through the brush.

Barbe stopped halfway to where Bloch lay and brought the gun to her shoulder. Iroedh drew her machete.

"There they come!" said Iroedh, pointing to where her dilated pupils made out a mass of moving figures.

Tactactactac! went the gun. In the lull following the uproar Iroedh heard sounds from the other direction and whirled. Three rogue drones were rushing upon the camp from that direction, spears poised. Iroedh stepped forward, bracing herself to meet the attack, though with such odds she was sure the moment would be her last.

Crack! went the pistol from where Bloch lay, and again. Bloch jumped up, grabbed the gun from Barbe, and fired another burst in yet a third direction. By the flashes Iroedh had a fleeting impression of bodies falling and others scampering back.

Bloch put one of the brass clips into the gun; then, eye to the night-seeing attachment, swept the device this way and that.

"They learn fast about taking cover," he said. "All out of sight but the stiffs."

From around the camp there now came a buzz and clatter of many people moving without trying to conceal the fact. Snatches of speech could be heard, and somewhere somebody moaned in pain.

Antis and Yaedh were up now, the former with his machete out. They all huddled in the midst of the crude barricade of baggage.

"I don't think they will try that again," said Bloch.

"Wythias is stubborn," said Yaedh. "His men fear him worse than they do your magic weapons."

"Yes, but can he make them attack if they won't? What's that?"

Something was happening down near the base of the slope, though Iroedh could not quite make out what. There were thumps and jinglings and footsteps.

Yaedh cried: "They're harnessing up the uegs! They will drive them off with our chariots!"

"Bless my soul!" said Bloch. "What shall we do?"

Antis said: "You could shoot in the general direction of the tethering place; that should get a few." He was sharpening his blade with a whetstone, *wheep-wheep.*

"But that would kill the uegs, and we should be almost as badly off as if they took them!"

"Then you could go down there with your gun and attack them at close range."

"Uh? I don't—I can't see as well in the dark, and there must be hundreds of them———"

98

"Are you afraid? Then I'll go after them with nothing but my matselh! I'll show——"

"There they go!" said Yaedh.

There was a cracking of whips and a shouting, and the sounds of receding chariotry.

"Too late," groaned Bloch. "Now we *are* in a fix! Our spare ammunition and food was in those chariots."

"And my biscuit flour," said Iroedh.

"And my notes," said Barbe.

Bloch said: "Yaedh, you speak their dialect. Ask them what they want."

Yaedh raised her head and called: "Wythias of Hawardem!"

After a few repetitions a voice called back: "I am speaking."

"What do you wish of us?"

"We wish the magical weapons of the Terrans. If they will give them up we will let you go."

When this had been translated, Bloch asked: "How reliable is this Wythias?"

"Not at all, seeing that he raises irreverent hands against a priestess of the Oracle."

Bloch hesitated, nervously cracking his knuckles. At last he said: "Tell him no. I couldn't face Subbarau if I let this fellow steal our guns."

Yaedh told Wythias no. There were more movements in the dark and then the hateful whistle of an arrow.

Bloch said: "Lie down inside your baggage, everybody!"

More arrows whistled; one struck the baggage with a sharp rap.

"Can't you see any of them in your magical viewer?" said Antis.

Bloch, who had been trying to do just that, replied: "Not enough for a shot. The archers are staying out of sight over the curvature of the hill and lofting them at us."

Iroedh said: "In that case they may not hit us."

"Maybe," said Bloch. "Keep down."

Antis said: "Why don't you creep out of here and attack them? If you got among them with that weapon you could slaughter them."

"I don't know . . . How many are there, Yaedh?"

"If the whole band is here, over two hundred," said the priestess.

The arrows continued to fall.

Bloch said: "Since they got our chariots I calculate I

have between eighty and a hundred rounds for the rifle, plus twenty or thirty for Barbe's pistol. With full-automatic fire you could shoot all that off in a matter of seconds, so we shall have to make every shot count. And you can see there are many more than I have cartridges."

It seemed to Iroedh that Bloch was trying to think up excuses for not getting any closer to the rogues. Antis persisted:

"If you killed a few, the rest would run. I'll go with you with my matselh——"

Yaedh gave a little shriek and a gasp. Iroedh, her shield slung across her back for protection, crept over to where the priestess lay with an arrow through her ribs. Yaedh sighed:

"If I could only have had a real love again in my life . . ."

Her head lolled. Iroedh said:

"She's dead, poor thing. Daktablak, I agree with Antis that there's no point in lying here the rest of the night under this arrow rain."

"Well?" said Bloch.

"I doubt if they have organized a tight circle around us yet. If we gathered up what we absolutely need and moved quietly we might burst through their line without their knowing it."

"I don't know——" said Bloch.

"She has reason," said Barbe.

"I hate to run away——" began Antis, but Barbe continued:

"We can go away from the road, which is the direction they won't expect, make a big semicircle and come back to the road several kilometers north of here, which should be near Ledhwid."

Arrows continued to fall.

"All right," said Bloch at last. "Everybody make a bundle of what he most needs. I suppose Barbe and I shall have to walk ahead with the guns, so you two Avtini will have to carry all the gear——"

"No," said Antis. "If you shoot those things the noise will tell the others what's happened. You carry the gear; Iroedh and I will walk ahead and——" He made a slashing motion.

Iroedh, fumbling in the dark, found she had comparatively few possessions. The only thing she really regretted was the biscuit flour, without which she foresaw a hungry time. She put her belongings into her cloak and tied the corners together as Antis was doing.

"Ready, everybody?" said Bloch. "Proceed quietly now!"

Crouching low and feeling their way along in single file, they issued from the remains of the baggage barricade and headed away from the road.

VIII. Royal Jelly

Antis led the way, shield before him and machete ready. Iroedh followed, looking over his shoulder. Behind them arrows continued to fall upon the deserted camp. Around them the creeping things kept up their symphony of night noises, and in the distance the rogues could be heard talking and moving.

They walked away from the road up the hill. Iroedh could hear the heavy breathing of the Terrans behind her; considering their loads it was not surprising.

Antis turned his head and made a tiny hiss. Iroedh crouched lower and moved more cautiously, fingering the hilt of her weapon.

A voice spoke in front of them: "Who is——"

As the dark shape materialized before them, Antis bounded forward and struck. Iroedh sprang after him, at an angle to bring her beside him, and swung too. She felt her blade bite into the unseen target.

The dark shape collapsed. When Bloch arrived, gun ready, the rogue lay dead.

"Come on," murmured Antis.

They went over the crest of the hill and down the other side. Here the trees began again, so they had to move with creeping slowness to avoid entanglement.

Bloch said: "Antis, can you see your way? How do you know you're not conducting us in a circle?"

"I don't know. I try to keep the sounds of the drones behind us."

"Suppose," said Bloch, "we open out to where I can barely perceive you. I'll sight on the girls and tell you whether you are bearing to one side or the other."

They tried this system, but without much success, because under the trees the darkness was too profound to see more than a few meters. After a while they adopted a more complicated scheme in which Bloch stood squinting through his infrared viewer while the others went ahead of him, obeying his instructions, and then they in turn stood still until he caught up with them. Where the brush was heavy Iroedh or Antis would go ahead to cut a way with a machete, all others staying well clear of the blade. Iroedh soon learned that her bronze replica of the implement did not hold an edge nearly so well as the steel original. In fact, after a couple of hours it was not much more effective than beating at the bushes with a bludgeon.

They were still struggling wearily ahead when the cloud canopy over the treetops lightened. Iroedh could never remember having been more tired; the tasks of a Community, while sometimes strenuous, were so organized as not to push the workers to exhaustion.

In the gray dawn they straggled out of the trees where a hillside rose in a bank of bare rock ledges. They climbed up these, ledge by ledge, until they were nearly at the top, then sat down to rest with their feet dangling.

Bloch said: "Have we anything to eat?"

Antis untied the corners of his cloak. "Of that stuff we brought from the chariots last night, only three containers were not opened. I brought them along. I think they're that soft oily meat you eat."

He held up three cans of tuna fish.

Barbe said: "How about the poor Iroedh?"

Bloch shrugged. "If she wants to take a chance on Terran fish, okay. Otherwise—— Is there no wild food in these woods?"

He opened one of the cans. Antis said:

"You can't easily live off this country. If I had your gun and knew how to use it, I might kill an occasional beast; but for her I don't know what there is."

"I've been looking," said Iroedh, "and the few edible berries and seeds found around Elham don't seem to grow this far north. No, I won't have any tunafyth, thank you. If we can get back to the road I'm sure I can hold out till we reach Ledhwid."

"If we can find the road again," said Barbe. "Winston, get out your map and compass."

Bloch got the map from his knapsack and unfolded it, then began hunting for his compass. He went through the knapsack, then through his pockets, his face registering deeper and deeper dismay.

"I'm sure I have it," he muttered.

102

Antis said: "That little round shiny thing you were looking at last night when you consulted the map? You laid it on the ground; perhaps you forgot to pick it up again."

Bloch went through everything again, then exclaimed: "That tears it! Barbe, why didn't you remind me? It's your business to see I don't forget things——"

"It is not! The last time I reminded you of such a thing you shut me up." Barbe turned to Iroedh. "It is a curious feature of Terran culture that when the men do something of a stupidity they always blame their wives."

"Huh," said Bloch. "Now we *are* in a predicament. If we had the sun I could tell north by my watch, and if we had the radio I could erect a directional loop and ascertain the direction of the *Paris*. As it is I haven't the faintest idea where we are or which way to proceed."

Iroedh said: "You have the map, haven't you?"

"Yes, but look at it!" He held it up. "It's a strip map of the route from Gliid to Ledhwid, made from a series of aerial photographs by Kang. All it shows is roads, streams, and a couple of Communities; the rest is forest. And since there aren't any signposts to tell us where we are on the map, all I know is we're somewhere to the east of the main road."

Antis said: "If we found a stream we could follow it down, don't you think?"

"Look!" said Barbe sharply.

Across the valley they faced, figures had appeared on the crest of the opposite hill. They were scattered over a wide front and popped in and out of sight as they moved through the vegetation. Although they were too far for features to be discerned, Iroedh saw that they carried spears.

Antis said: "Let's run for it."

"No!" said Bloch. "Sit absolutely still. If we don't move they may not observe us."

They sat frozen while the first group of drones disappeared into the heavier cover of the lower slope and more came into view on the crest.

Barbe said: "At this rate the first ones will have come up to us before the last ones have come over the hilltop."

"Oh!" said Iroedh. "I think they see us."

There was a scurry of motion among the approaching drones, with much shouting and pointing. Those in sight broke into a run.

Bloch groaned. "Off we go! Don't cut any brush, Antis; it'll give them a trail to follow."

They got to their feet and scrambled up the slope and into the woods again.

"I wonder," panted Barbe, "how they—found us—this time?"

Antis answered: "They do much hunting—and some—are expert trackers. And we did—cut a lot—of brush."

Iroedh saved her breath for hiking, feeling weak from lack of food. They ran when the terrain permitted, otherwise walked as fast as they could. On and on, without any particular attention to direction. Sometimes Bloch led, sometimes Antis. Anything to put distance between themselves and the band.

Iroedh discarded her helmet and buckler (obtained from the dead drones the previous day) to the annoyance of Antis, who, during his sojourn with Umwys, seemed to have become a connoisseur of arms and armor, and hence resented having to give up a good piece.

At last Barbe said: "It must that I—stop for a minute."

As they stood panting, the hallooing of the pursuit came faintly. Off they went again.

Bloch said: "Yaedh was correct; that Wythias lusts after these guns in the worst way."

"Naturally," said Antis. "He could rule the planet with them."

"Not without ammunition, but perhaps he doesn't know that. Can you go now, Barbe?"

On and on. To Iroedh the flight became a nightmare of running, walking, climbing over logs and rocks, stumbling, falling down, getting up again, and stumbling on some more. All day they hiked, and most of the night.

In the afternoon of the next day they came to a stream. Bloch said:

"If we wade up or down this we may throw them off our trail."

They splashed along the stream bed for half a borb until the stream began to curve around in the direction from which they had come. Bloch, leading, turned his head back to say:

"I think we should take the woods again—— *Wup!*"

His legs had suddenly sunk into the stream bed up to the knees, and the rest of him seemed to be following.

"Quicksand!" he yelled. "Somebody shove me a pole!" He peeled off his knapsack and threw it ashore. "Barbe, catch the gun!"

Iroedh was so exhausted that she could only stand and stare stupidly while Antis stumbled ashore and began looking for a sapling to cut. It seemed, however, that all the trees in this section were old forest giants. While Antis was still searching, Barbe got down on hands and knees and crawled out over the sand of the bottom toward where Bloch was already in up to his waist.

"Catch this!" she said, swinging her jacket toward him, holding it by one sleeve. After a couple of tries he caught it.

Iroedh pulled herself together and hurried to grasp Barbe's ankles to keep her from going in too. Little by little, holding first the jacket and then Barbe's hand, Bloch wallowed shoreward. By the time Antis showed up with a pole Bloch was safe, and a few seconds later was sitting on a rock digging the mud out of his ears while Barbe kissed him and told him how wonderful he was.

Iroedh, though she listened, could hear no sounds of pursuit. Bloch said:

"We may have eluded them. If we can find another pool further down, we might get cleaned up a little before taking to the woods again."

They continued on down, avoiding the quicksand, and soon came to another pool in which they removed the mud from their clothes and persons. Iroedh noted that the curious exposure tabu of the Terrans seemed to be in abeyance, or perhaps it did not apply to mated persons. One Terran stood guard while the other washed. Iroedh stared at them with frank physiological interest, noting resemblances and differences between man and Avtin and speculating about their significance. As the resemblances outweighed the differences, she guessed that biological fundamentals must be much the same in the two species.

Then off into the woods they went again. By nightfall they agreed that they had probably lost their pursuers. The only trouble was that they had also lost themselves in the process, even more thoroughly than before.

"If we could only get some sun," said Bloch, "we could hike north a few borbi, then west again, and pick up the road in a couple of days . . . Oh-oh, rain!"

A pattering on the leaves overhead made itself heard. Bloch asked:

"How long is a rain likely to last hereabouts?"

Antis shrugged. "Perhaps an hour, perhaps three or four days."

"Everything happens to us," said Bloch. "All we need now is for one of your noags to try to devour us."

"Don't say that!" said Antis. "There are those who believe that saying such a thing makes it come true.

Besides, in these northern woods the noags grow to much greater size than around Elham."

"Anyway, we might bestir ourselves to construct a shelter," said Bloch. "Iroedh, if you'll cut some poles . . ."

Iroedh tried to get to her feet, but to her consternation found she could not.

"I can't get up," she said. "I'm too weak."

"Running all that distance on an empty stomach, it's no wonder," said Barbe.

Bloch said: "Lend me your machete, then," and went off with Antis. Iroedh could hear them blundering about and slashing, but was too far gone to care whether she acquired shelter from the rain or not.

"This becomes serious, my little," said Barbe. "Even if the rain stops it will take us two or three days to get back to the road, and how will you manage without food?"

"I—I think I could get up now," said Iroedh. "I shall be better when I've rested."

The shelter took gradual form, though so much water dripped through the greenery that served as a thatch that Iroedh found it but little improvement on no shelter. Bloch, Barbe, and Antis divided the remaining tuna. Not wishing to show a light, they forewent a fire and prepared to make the best of a dank and miserable night. Antis produced his telh and began tweedling, whereupon Bloch exclaimed:

"Do you mean to say that when we were fleeing for our lives we were hauling *that* piece of junk?"

Antis replied with hauteur: "Daktablak, I made no objections when you brought along your mouth furnace and a goodly supply of the weed you burn in it."

Bloch looked at his freshly lit pipe and changed the subject.

The rain continued another day and another night, and yet another day and another night. Then it ceased as a brisk cool wind soughed through the treetops and blew away the cloud cover. Bloch hurried over to the first patch of sunlight, performed magical rites with his watch and a knife blade, and triumphantly announced:

"That's north! Let's go!"

Iroedh found that her two days' rest had given her some strength to go on—at least for a time. But the going proved harder, for now that he knew his direction, Bloch insisted upon the party's sticking close to it, even though it forced them to scramble over steep hogbacks and splash through black bogs where small creeping and flying things

106

bit and stung, instead of following the line of least resistance as they had been doing. They marched all day, camped, and next day marched again.

During the morning they climbed out of one swamp hole and up the face of a steep hill. Presently they surmounted a ledge projecting from the side of the hill. Above the ledge the rock overhung to make a cave which, while shallow, was quite big enough to accommodate the four of them. By common consent they all sank down upon the ledge to rest. Antis, as usual, took advantage of the pause to whet his and Iroedh's machetes, while Bloch swept the sky with his binoculars for a sight of Kang.

Bloch, on whose lower face a growth of yellow-brown hair was sprouting, said: "This would have been a much more comfortable place to spend those two rainy days, but I suppose—— What's that?"

An animal had come out of the woods: a bipedal herbivore like an ueg but bigger. It was peacefully breaking off the branches of trees with its hands and eating the leaves.

Antis said: "That's a pandre-eg, a wild relative of the ueg. Kill it, quickly!"

"Is it dangerous?" whispered Barbe.

"No, but I'm starved."

Bang! Iroedh leaped with fright. When the ringing in her ears subsided she saw that the pandre-eg had fallen to the ground, kicking and thrashing. Bloch leaped down the slope. As he neared the beast it stopped moving.

"Dinner!" he called.

The other three trooped down to where the animal lay. Bloch said:

"I should like to save it as a specimen, of course, but I'm afraid——"

"Oh, you!" said Barbe. "You're as bad with your specimens as Antis with his armor."

"Can you butcher this thing, Antis?" said Bloch.

"With pleasure. I learned how from Umwys. However, it will save time if you'll lend me that knife of Terran metal. Oh, Iroedh!"

"Yes?"

"How does that hunter's dance go when you wish to change your luck?"

"You set a game animal's head on a stake and dance naked eight times around it sunwise, facing backwards. If you fall down or see a khal tree it spoils it and you have to start over."

107

"There don't seem to be any khal trees," said Antis, "so take off your boots. We're going to try it."

Antis began sawing on the beast's neck while Iroedh unlaced her boots, finding that it took all her strength to do so. The prospect of dancing eight times around anything appalled her, especially as she doubted whether it would actually work. On the other hand, she was a little afraid of offending Antis.

Bloch had spread a cloth on the ledge and taken his gun apart, laying the parts out in careful order and cleaning and oiling each one. Barbe went for water, using Antis's helmet as a bucket.

"There!" said Antis, forcing the pandre-eg's head down upon the point of the stake he had whittled. Blood trickled down the stake.

Bloch said: "It seems to me your magical rite is a trifle confused. Presumably it's to transform a hunter's bad luck to good—that is, to let him kill game. But if it has to be performed with a game animal's head, that means his luck has already turned."

"You don't understand these matters, Daktablak," said Antis. "It always works for us. Are you ready, beautiful?"

Iroedh got up slowly. "I'm so tired, Antis . . ."

"It will only take a minute. Come on, you stand on that side while I stand on this. Ready?"

He began clapping his hands together and hopping backwards. Iroedh, staggering, did likewise. On the third time around she tripped and sat down.

"Iroedh!" cried Antis with unconcealed exasperation. "Now we shall have to begin over. Try to keep glancing back over your shoulder, won't you? That's a brave worker."

They got up to six circuits of the head when two pistol shots cracked. Barbe appeared, running, and behind her came a noag—a monster of its species, half again as tall as a person. Its long neck arched, its jaws gaped, its clawed hands reached out, and its long tail stuck up behind like a guidon.

"Run!" screamed Barbe, coming toward them.

Bloch jumped to his feet on the ledge, holding his useless gun barrel.

"Up here!" he bawled. "We can hold it off!"

Iroedh summoned her last ounce of strength to scramble up the short slope to the ledge. Antis dashed ahead of her; then, seeing her falter, caught her arm and hauled her after him.

A despairing scream from Barbe made Iroedh look

back. The female man had almost reached the foot of the slope when she had tripped and fallen prone. The pistol, which she had been carrying in her hand, bounced along the ground ahead of her. The noag came on in great bounding strides.

Something went past Iroedh in a brown blur. It was Bloch, holding the machete Antis had left on the ledge over his head and uttering a Terran war cry that sounded like *"Sanavabyts! Sanavabyts!"*

The noag, stooping to seize Barbe, looked up and backed away with a startled snarl as this new antagonist hurled himself at it. The machete whirled in circles of light; the noag screamed as the blade sheared off two clawed fingers and bit into the fanged muzzle. Antis, seeing what was up, picked up Iroedh's machete from the ground and started toward the scene of the fight. Before he arrived, the noag, slashed and bloody, had turned to run. With a last cut Bloch took off the tip of its tail. The noag disappeared, its howls coming back fainter and fainter until they could no longer be heard.

Then Bloch and Barbe were embracing and uttering Terran endearments. Antis, watching, said to Iroedh:

"I misjudged Daktablak, thinking he lacked courage. That took nerve and quick wit, don't you think?"

Iroedh herself admitted that in the conflicts with the drones Bloch had acted rather uncertain, disorganized, and timid. She said:

"It must be that Terran love of theirs. Remember the quicksand? Whatever troubles it may cause, that kind of love makes them run risks for each other they wouldn't for anybody else."

When Bloch, Barbe, and Antis had eaten their fill of pandre-eg steak, Bloch said: "Shall we rest in the cave for a while to get our strength back, or go on right now and cover as much ground as we can before dark?"

Antis was for pushing on; Barbe for resting some more. When they turned to Iroedh she said:

"It makes no difference to me because I cannot go on in any case."

"Why not?" said Bloch.

Barbe said: "The poor thing is weak from the starvation, that's why not. Look at her ribs. She's had nothing to eat for six days, most of it climbing around this terrible country."

Iroedh said: "I'm ashamed to admit it, but that is the

truth. The rest of you go on whenever you like; I'm done for."

"Nonsense!" said Barbe. "Do you think we would leave you here to die?"

"There is no point in your dying too. Go on."

"I wouldn't leave you, beautiful," said Antis. "You are all I love."

"If you love me you will save yourself. I can't go on, and that's that."

"We could carry you," said Antis.

"No, you couldn't in this rough country. I should probably be dead before you reached the road, and what good would it do to burden yourselves? Think of me as dead already, as if the noag had slain me, and make our parting as painless as possible."

Antis said: "Even if I knew you were going to die, I'd stay with you to the end."

"And have the rogue drones catch you? Don't be irrational. I'll kill myself before I let you do that."

"We'll see that you have nothing sharp."

"There are other ways. And what's the sense of it? You didn't make such a fuss over poor Yaedh."

"That was different," said Barbe. "She was dead already, and we never felt toward her as we do toward you. You are like one of us—one of our Terran kind, I mean."

Bloch spoke up: "I think we're interring Iroedh before there's any necessity. All she requires is a few good meals."

"And where shall I find those?" said Iroedh, with barely the strength to talk.

Bloch gestured toward the eviscerated remains of the pandre-eg.

"You know I cannot eat meat," said Iroedh. "It would poison me."

"Have you ever eaten it?" asked Bloch.

"No."

"Have you ever known an Avtiny worker who had?"

"No. They wouldn't have been alive for me to know them."

"Well, if you think you're going to perish anyway, why not try it? At worst it can only kill you a little sooner, and at best it might give you the strength to persevere."

"But it's such a painful death!"

"I'll make an agreement with you. You eat a steak, and if I see you dying in convulsions I'll blow your brains out with the pistol. You'll never know what struck you."

As Iroedh hesitated, turning this drastic proposal over

110

in her mind, Bloch continued: "Come on, what have you to lose? Either way it's better than waiting for one of those Jabberwocks to devour you——"

"Those what?"

"Jabberwock, a monster out of Terran folklore. I thought the noag looked a little like one. What about a steak?"

Antis said: "I don't know. I favor her trying the meat, but I couldn't stand by and watch you slay her in cold blood."

"No, Antis," said Iroedh weakly. "The Terran is right. Cook me up a piece and I will try it."

A few minutes later Iroedh picked up a slab of steak, blew on her fingers as it scorched them, and turned it over warily.

"Go on," said Bloch. "A nice big bite."

Iroedh opened her mouth, then lost her courage and closed it again. She gathered her forces, drew a long breath, shut her eyes, and sank her teeth into the meat.

A lifetime of conditioning caused her to gag and retch, but her shrunken stomach contained nothing to vomit. She clamped her jaws firmly shut until her gorge subsided, then forced herself to chew.

At first she thought it tasted vile. Then she was not sure whether she liked it or not. It was so *different* from anything she had ever eaten. She got her first bite down and took a second.

"Good for you!" said Bloch. "No pains?"

"No, but they wouldn't have started yet. It is not so bad as I thought."

They watched her in silence as she finished the piece.

"Do you know," she said, "I think I could eat another. Not that I really like it, but I'm still hungry, and I might as well die on a full stomach."

"Wait a while," said Bloch. "Too much after a fast like yours *would* upset you. And it's so late now we might as well spend the night here."

They made what camp they could and did a more thorough job on the pandre-eg, burying the guts and mounting the more edible parts on stakes. Antis, indicating the head which still grinned gruesomely at them from its stake, said:

"We never did finish our good-luck dance. Iroedh . . . ?"

Iroedh put up a firm hand. "My love, if it were a matter of saving our whole race from extinction I couldn't dance one step. If you must dance, why not ask the Terrans?"

111

"Oh, very well. How about it, Barbe?"

"How about what?"

Antis explained about the good-luck dance. Barbe first burst out laughing, to the obvious perplexity of Antis. Then she said:

"Well—I should like to, me, but I don't know . . ."

She cast a questioning look at Bloch, who said: "Go right ahead, my dear. It's part of our job to participate in Ormazdian activities when opportunity offers. Besides, with his cultural attitudes I doubt if Antis would know what a *voyeur* was."

"What a what was?" said Antis.

"A Terran organism noted for its keenness of vision. Go on, his dancing can't be worse than mine."

Barbe caught her bare heels and sat down twice in the course of the good-luck dance, which made the wearily watching Iroedh feel somehow better.

At sunset they ate again. Iroedh, whose mind had been nervously exploring her viscera ever since her heretical meal, said:

"There's no sign of trouble yet. There must be something wrong with me, or I should be writhing in my death throes."

"Or something wrong with your system of tabus," said Bloch. "Have some more?"

"By Gwyyr, I will!"

Next morning they impaled all the meat they could carry on a long pole, which Bloch and Antis carried slung between them over their shoulders. They started down the slope into the woods. Iroedh, marching ahead of them, felt much stronger in body but bewildered in mind. Could all workers eat meat with impunity? Then why on Niond had such a rule or belief been set up in the first place?

She was thinking along these lines when a cry and the sound of a fall made her turn. Barbe lay at the base of the slope, holding her ankle. Her face was pale.

"Sprained it," she said.

Bloch hurried back and helped his mate take off her boot. He felt the ankle while Barbe went "Ow!"

Bloch sighed. "I presume we shall spend another day here at least; she can't walk now. Next time we're ready to start, no doubt Antis will cut himself open with his own machete, or I shall get careless and shoot off my big toe. So much for your good-luck ritual, Antis."

"You can't tell," said Antis. "Without the dance who

112

knows what might have happened? She might have broken her leg instead of merely wrenching it."

"Merely wrenching it!" said Barbe between clenched teeth.

"An unanswerable sophistry, my friend," said Bloch. "Take her other arm."

They helped Barbe back on to the ledge and settled down again. To put the time to good use Bloch interrogated Iroedh some more about her native world. Barbe took notes in her notebook, and when she ran out of paper Antis found a vakhwil tree and peeled off enough bark to keep Barbe supplied for several days with writing material. Iroedh, eating regularly again, got stronger fast.

Barbe's sprain, however, proved more serious than they had thought. Her ankle swelled to twice its normal size and turned an assortment of greens and purples. Bloch said:

"We may be here for a week, so I'd better hunt some more food. That pandre-eg will soon begin to stink."

And off he went with Antis.

Six days later Iroedh sat on the ledge and watched Barbe try her ankle in gingerly fashion. The males were off hunting again. Iroedh felt in need of advice but did not quite know how to go about getting it. The personnel officer of Elham, who normally handled personal problems, was many borbi away. Moreover, one of the things bothering Iroedh was that her dreams had been taking such strange forms that she was embarrassed to submit them. For instance there was the dream about the memorial pillar in the ruins of Khinam that behaved as no normal pillar should. Then there was the curious feeling of anger that possessed her when Antis artlessly bragged about his proficiency in fulfilling his function as Queen Intar's drone. Finally, she seemed to be undergoing other changes almost too bizarre for belief.

Barbe said: "I think if I give it a little of the exercise today I may be able to hike tomorrow, or the next day at the latest."

"The swelling is nearly gone," said Iroedh. "And speaking of swelling——"

"Yes, my dear?"

"It's hard to know where to begin, but as another female I thought you might understand."

"Understand what?"

"Ever since I started eating meat I have had the oddest sensations."

113

"Such as?"

"Well—for instance, there's a feeling of tightness in the skins of my chest. And when I look down I could swear my breasts are getting larger, like those of a functional female. Is it my imagination?"

Barbe gave Iroedh's figure a sharp look. "No, it isn't. You definitely bulge."

"And I have peculiar internal feelings, too, as if other organs were growing."

Barbe said: "Turn around. I can't see inside you, of course, but your hips do look wider."

"But what shall I *do?*"

"What do you mean? You are doing all right, aren't you?"

"I can't turn into a functional female!"

"And why not?" said Barbe.

"It's unheard-of! I should be a monstrosity!"

"Well, if you are bound to become a monstrosity, why not relax and enjoy the role?"

"It must be the meat. But if I stop eating it I shall die!"

"And there wouldn't be any fun to that, would there? You just go right ahead, dear little monster. We shall love you in all cases."

When Bloch and Antis came back to the cave with a leipag the former had shot, Barbe made the announcement.

Bloch said: "Bless my soul! That's the best thing since Antis sat on the dhug and we had to pull the spines out of his podex."

"You know, darling," said Antis, "I *thought* something was happening to you. What's the cause of this change, Daktablak?"

Bloch lighted his pipe before answering. "You wouldn't know about hormones, but they are substances in your blood that make you grow up and develop in various directions. At least I suppose you have them just as we do, since your body chemistry seems to be similar to ours.

"Now, one set of hormones controls development of sexual characteristics, and apparently among the Avtini the glands that secrete these hormones require meat in the diet to function. So the workers feed meat to drones and queens and deny it to those they intend to develop into workers. It's like the bees on Terra who feed certain larvae"—he had to stop to explain what bees and larvae were—"who feed certain larvae a special food called 'royal jelly' that causes them to develop into queens."

Antis said: "Does that mean a drone fed on an all-plant diet would also become a neuter worker?"

"I don't know," said Bloch, but Barbe put in:

"Don't you remember that visitor from Khwiem, who told us of the Community of Arsuuni who prefer neuter-male Avtiny slaves to the usual neuter-female ones? We thought she meant they make eunuchs of them, but it may be they simply rear drone children on a diet without meat."

"Conceivably," said Bloch.

Antis asked: "Then *must* drones and queens be reared on a completely meat diet? Or could they live on a mixed diet as you do?"

"You could ascertain that by trying plant food, though I wouldn't guarantee results. My own surmise is that, considering the abnormally high egg-laying capacity of your queens, they're oversexed as a result of an unmixed meat diet. The males I wouldn't even guess about."

Iroedh wailed: "But what will happen to me?"

Bloch blew a smoke ring. "Well, my dear, I don't see that you'll be any worse off than you are, and you may enjoy some new experiences."

"There won't be any place for me on Niond. Would Captain Subbarau employ Antis and me in his crew?"

"No. It's against I.C. policy to transport natives of Class H planets off their own worlds. But you'll make out, I'm certain. Funny; I once read about a young lady named Alice who became a queen by jumping over a brook, but this is the first time I ever heard of one's becoming a queen by eating steak three times a day!"

IX. The Oracle

Once again on their way, they camped by a small stream and devoured a portion of the meat they had brought from the cave. Bloch said:

"I've been wondering how a band as large as that of Wythias manages. The hunting doesn't seem good enough in these parts to feed so many in one area."

"I've heard," said Antis, "that northwest of Ledhwid Wythias has land of his own where he raises the food he needs."

"It would require a hell of a big ranch to provide steaks for all those brigands. I wonder if perhaps they don't subsist on a mixed diet despite your tabus?"

"What makes you think that?"

"Because you can get a lot more calories from a given area by using vegetable crops directly than by feeding them to animals and eating the animals . . ."

Iroedh, finishing her steak, hardly heard the discussion, which wandered off into the technicalities of dietetics. She was more concerned with her own problems.

For one thing, her change of shape did not altogether suit her. Her new mammae bounced and jiggled in a ridiculous manner when she ran, and she was sure the thickening of her body through the pelvic region was making her less agile. At first she had thought this thickening a mere deposit of fat, but now it seemed that the actual bone structure was spreading as well. The Avtiny neuter-female worker's body was built to an admirably functional design, with a minimum of vulnerable projections; but this awkward thing . . .

Then there was the strange attitude of Antis. On one hand he had taken to staring at her in a curiously intent fashion when he thought she was not looking. Time and again she caught him at it, and he would at once look away and pretend he had been observing something else all the time. On the other hand he developed an odd standoffishness, refusing to sleep with her any more on the mumbled pretext that he was not getting enough actual sleep.

What on Niond was bothering the dear fellow? Iroedh for her part loved him more than ever and wanted to be close to him as much as possible. She found herself, in fact, developing a possessive, sentimental, and exclusive tenderness toward him like that attributed to the females in *A Girl of the Limberlost* toward their drones.

It was very puzzling. Why had all this happened to her? In the old days, according to her researches, one blamed a jealous or capricious god for one's undeserved misfortunes, but nobody had taken the gods seriously for generations. It was, thinkers agreed, a case of the mysterious operations of luck. Emotionally, however, blind chance was a poor substitute for a god when you wanted something on which to turn your resentment at the hard treatment accorded you by fate . . .

116

"Hey, Iroedh!" said Bloch. "Turn in! You have third watch."

Iroedh pulled herself together. "Antis . . . ?"

Antis scowled. "If you don't mind," he said, indicating the far side of the open space.

"But why? I shall be cold and lonesome. Are you angry? What have I done?"

"On the contrary . . ." Antis seemed torn by indecision, then burst out: "You forget you're now a queen, Iroedh dearest."

"Oh, but not yet!"

"Well then, a princess. A functional female. In fact we ought to call you 'Iroer,' except that we're used to the old name."

"What of it? Do you love me less because of it?"

"Not at all. But I'm a functional male, do you see? And if I may not act like one . . ."

"Why can't you?" she asked innocently.

"You mean—you mean with *you?*"

"Of course, stupid. You certainly boast enough about yourself and that bloated old Intar. Am I less attractive than she?"

"Oh, darling, there's no comparison. But—you see, then I was acting under orders. I shouldn't know how to take the initiative in such a case. I don't know what to do. If you were just any old queen, I'd—— But you're Iroedh, whom I've always looked up to like one of the old goddesses. You're so much more intelligent than I——"

"I'm not really—"

"Don't contradict!" he roared.

Iroedh was surprised, first by his vehemence, second by the fact that she did not mind being bossed so much as she would have before her change. (That cursed diet again!)

Antis, looking at her sharply, continued: "Does this mean you're planning to collect yourself a harem of drones like other queens?"

"I don't know. I hadn't thought. I suppose so. Why, have you any objections?"

"I certainly have! You're mine by right of discovery or something, and I've had my fill of sharing my queen with a dozen others. If I catch another drone so much as looking at you, I'll serve him as King Aithles used Idhios in the *Lay.*"

"Are you sure you can minister to the needs of a whole functional female all by yourself, when the task is normally divided among twelve or sixteen drones?"

"Certainly. I could take care, not only of you, but of

117

two or three functional females at once. If I had a couple here——"

"I like that! You wish me to have no drones but you, yet you reserve the right to fertilize any queen who falls into your clutches."

"Don't you think I should?"

"I don't know whether you should or not, but it would make me just as unhappy as my entertaining other drones would make you."

Antis stared at the fire, chewing a stick for some seconds, then said: "I suppose we need some definite agreement, like that which we drones enter into when we reach our majority. Now, the Terrans have worked out a system of male-plus-female units, based upon their long experience, which seems to work for them. According to what you tell me, our remote ancestors had such a system before the reforms of Danoakor and the rest. But that's gone and forgotten, so that we should have to start practically from nothing. I think we might ask the advice of our Terran friends."

"I was about to suggest the same thing! Oh, Daktablak!"

"Yes?"

Antis and Iroedh, speaking alternate paragraphs, explained their predicament.

Bloch ran his fingers through his stubble of beard. "Bless my soul! Don't tell me you two are in love in the full, ghastly, sentimental Terran sense?"

"It looks that way," said Antis, "as far as we can judge. To me it's like being on fire."

"It's got you," said Bloch. "If Mrs. Porter could only know the revolutionary effect of her sentimental potboiler on the culture of a planet eight light-years away and nearly three centuries after her time——"

"But what shall we *do?*" pleaded Iroedh.

"Why, of course you—that is—— How should I know? What do you desire to do?"

Iroedh spoke: "We should like to be like you and Barbe."

"Well, what hinders you? I suppose you know the mechanics of——"

Antis said: "Daktablak, you don't understand. With you Terrans mating is not a mere animal act, but an institution. Now, we have no such institution on Niond, but we should like one. If we're starting a new way of life we wish to start it right, and therefore we pick the best model we know: your system."

118

"Your confidence in Terran institutions touches me, my dear friends, and I hope it is not too badly misplaced. Apparently you wish me to devise, offhand, an institution of marriage for your whole race: a task to daunt the boldest. Have you considered that you belong to a species different from ours; that your cultural background differs greatly from ours; and that therefore a system that worked passably well for us might not function so well with you?"

Iroedh said: "We have to start somewhere, and if we make mistakes we can correct them as they arise."

"Wouldn't it be better to wait a few days until we consult the Oracle? You will have a clearer idea of your destinies——"

Barbe broke in: "Stop making excuses, Winston darling. You know you don't take this old Oracle seriously. Besides, we may all be dead in a few days."

"I just wanted to be sure they realized——"

"*Ils y ont mûrement réfléchi.* Go ahead, marry them."

Bloch sighed, "Apparently I'm elected Justice of the Peace for the planet Ormazd. It may be legally invalid and sociologically imprudent, but you're three to one against me. Antis, what do you Avtini swear by when you testify to the truth of an assertion?"

"One swears by one's Community, but we have no——"

"Wait," said Iroedh. "There is an old form of oath, now obsolete, by the gods Dhiis and Tiwinos and Eunmar and Gwyyr and the rest. It was used up to a few years ago in some conservative Communities, even though the swearers no longer believed in the gods."

"We'll employ that, then," said Bloch. "Now on Terra the agreement is exclusive and (at least nominally) for life, though in some cases provision is made——"

"Oh, we want it for life!" said Antis. "Don't you, beautiful?"

"Y-yes," said Iroedh, "though it does seem to me that some provision should be made in case the drone's fertility and other powers decline——"

"Listen," said Bloch, "I'm taking a big chance in devising a marriage system for you, and I'm damned if I will also commit myself to the task of formulating a divorce law. You let that work itself out. Barbe, what can you remember of that service Subbarau tied us with?"

Iroedh subsided, not without some inner reservations.

In time they got the wordings straightened out, and Bloch said: "Repeat after me: I, Antis of Elham, a functional male, take you, Iroedh of Elham, a functional female, to be my permanent and exclusive mate, to have and to hold . . ."

". . . and the curious thing is," said Iroedh to Barbe, "that whereas I used to be the dominant one of the pair, Antis now makes all the decisions. Of course I know more of the world than he, and he knows I do, so we play a little game. I make a suggestion—very tentatively, so as not to sound as if I were commanding him—and he grunts and says he'll think about it. Then next day he bursts out: 'Beautiful, I've just had the most wonderful idea!' and goes on to repeat my suggestion in the very words I used. Isn't it amazing?"

"Not so amazing to me as it seems to you," replied Barbe. "On the whole do you like our one-mate system?"

Iroedh did a couple of steps from a round dance. "Like it! It is wonderful! I've given up even the thought of a harem of drones, for while it's too early to tell about Antis's fertility, I'm sure no mate could give me more pleasure."

"Winston would say that was not a scientific attitude, but sometimes an unscientific attitude is better."

"Of course," continued Iroedh, "now that I'm getting to know Antis really well I realize he has faults along with his virtues. He's headstrong, irritable, sometimes inconsiderate, and often pompous where his own dignity is concerned. But he's honest and brave and jolly, so I still adore him."

"Oh, they all have faults. My man, for instance, is clever as anything, but he is basically weak, that one, and has moods of depression in which he's no good for sex or anything else."

"Really? I hadn't noticed."

"You wouldn't. They try to hide these failings from everybody except their wives. But if we wait around for the perfect mate we shall be in a deep hole before we find him. Allô, what is this?"

They had come out on to the road to Ledhwid about a day later than they expected, and had now been marching north on this road for some hours, with their remaining belongings in bundles on the ends of sticks they bore on their shoulders. Although the road was rough, it seemed easy to Iroedh after the endless cross-country scramble she had experienced. The hills were getting steeper and less densely wooded; right now the road was heading into a great gorge, which Iroedh knew by repute as the Gorge of Hwead. Ledhwid could not be much farther.

The cause of Barbe's exclamation was a corpse—or rather skeleton—lying by the road. A little further on lay another, and she saw still others scattered among the bushes and boulders. They had lain there long enough for the scavenger beasts to have picked the bones fairly clean, so that the stench of death had almost disappeared, but not so long but that occasional scraps of skin and cloth lingered among the remains.

"Iroedh!" cried Bloch. "Come here and identify these for me!"

He bounded up among the rocks to where a cuirass and helmet, dulled but not yet badly corroded, lay among a litter of bones.

Iroedh climbed up after him and said: "Let me see the teeth. That's an Avtiny worker; from the device on the helmet she would have been from Khwiem." She went from skeleton to skeleton. "All seem to be workers from the northern Communities. No, here's a drone, also an Avtin. I thought this might be a massacre by a war party of Arsuuni, but to judge from the remains and the weapons it was an attack on a party of workers from several Communities by a band of rogue Avtiny drones. Probably the band of Wythias. The news of this slaughter had not yet reached Elham when I left there, but news travels slowly."

Bloch said: "It's that tightly compartmented society of yours. I wish I could take some of these stiffs along; I've been wanting an Avtiny skeleton in the worst way."

"You're not going to collect a series now!" cried Barbe.

"N-no, though I would if we had transport. I'll merely take this one skull along to study on the way."

He hopped from rock to rock back to the road, precariously balancing the round white object on the palm of one hand. The journey resumed.

Iroedh said: "What on Niond do you want with a lot of old bones?"

"To learn how the life forms on Niond are built, and how they evolved," said Bloch.

"How they *what?*"

"Evolved." Bloch gave a short account of the evolutionary process.

"By Gwyyr, that's not what I learned in the filiary! We were taught that the world was hatched from an egg."

"You may think as you please," said Bloch. "However, do you know of any place where bones are found imbedded in rock or earth?"

"Yes; in Thidhem there's a cliff, worn away by wind

121

and weather, where such bones are exposed. Do you wish such things?"

"I certainly do. We need such bones, called 'fossils,' to learn how a race of egg-laying mammals evolved into organisms much like ourselves."

Barbe remarked: "It is not so strange; much the same thing happened on Krishna, and we have the platypus on Earth ... This road seems very little used; we've seen nobody except that one cart that passed us an hour ago."

"It's Wythias's band," explained Antis. "While they're out, all the Communities in their path keep their workers at home."

They were now well into the Gorge of Hwead. Bloch looked nervously up at the towering walls and said:

"This would be a fine place to drop rocks on people below." Later he added: "What's that noise? Like bells."

Iroedh listened too. "It is bells; the bells of Ledhwid. They're hung from the branches of the sacred grove and are rung by the wind, and the Oracle interprets the sounds."

Bloch murmured a Terran poem:

" 'Tis mute, the word they went to hear on high Dodona
    Mountain
When winds were in the oakenshaws and all the caul-
    drons tolled ..."

The Gorge of Hwead opened out and there stood the Hill of Ledhwid, crowned by the sacred grove of trees of immense size and antiquity. Before the grove, at the top of the path that wound up the steep hillside, stood the temple, of translucent blue stone, massive and graceful at the same time.

"Bless my soul!" said Bloch. "Whoever built that structure knew his business. I wish we hadn't donated our camera to Wythias."

"The ancients built such things," said Iroedh. "Perhaps if Antis and I can start some people living as they did, we shall be able to do as well again."

They straggled up the path to the irregular chiming of the bells. The slope made them puff. Iroedh looked down distastefully at her shape and for an instant resented her new weight; then remembered that without all this she and Antis would never have been united. That was worth hauling any number of bothersome female organs!

They passed through a gate in the stone wall that ran around the whole top of the hill. In front of the temple

122

stood a single Avtiny worker-guard in such finery as Iroedh had never seen, even on a queen. Her cuirass and helmet seemed to be of gold, and the latter bore a rim of jewels with a big glittering stone in front, faceted like that in Barbe's engagement ring.

"Good afternoon, sister," said Bloch. "I wonder if——"

"You are expected," said the guard. "Oh, Garnedh! Conduct these two visitors of another race to the Oracle at once. You two"—she indicated the Avtini—"will have to send in your question in the usual form."

"But they're with me——" began Bloch.

"I'm sorry, but I have my orders. Garnedh will take care of you."

The other guard, who had stepped out of the shadows inside the temple, led Bloch and Barbe away. Iroedh, feeling lost, sat down on the steps. Antis relaxed against a pillar and blew on his flute a bar of an ancient Terran song Bloch had taught them, one that began:

"Main aidh av siin dhe glory av dhe kamyng av dhe Lord . . ."

"Antis," said Iroedh, "what's this 'usual form' in which they wish questions submitted?"

"I can tell you that," said the guard. "Write your question on this pad, giving your name and Community, and send it in with your offering."

"Offering?"

"Certainly. You don't suppose an institution like this runs on air, do you?"

Iroedh looked at Antis. "I have nothing to offer, darling,"

"Neither have I——"

"How about some of that handsome armor of yours?" Iroedh turned to the guard. "Would his helmet be acceptable?"

"Quite," said the guard.

"Hey!" cried Antis. "I won't give up my armor! We may yet have a battle on our hands."

"But then how shall we submit a question?"

"We needn't. We know what's good for us as well as the Oracle does."

The guard said: "There is one other course: to submit a report on your Community. If you will write several thousand words on everything that has happened there recently, as well as any other news you have picked up along the way, the Master may consider that an acceptable substitute." The guard's voice became confidential. "My dear, I hope you won't consider me inquisitive, but you're a queen, aren't you?"

"You might say so."

"Well, this is something I have never seen in all my years of service here! Are you fleeing the destruction of your Community by the Arsuuni, or what?"

"No. I'm an ex-worker."

"Impossible! Or should I say a miracle? May I make your acquaintance, Queen? I am Ystalverdh of Thidhem."

"I'm Iroedh of Elham—or was. And this is Antis of Elham."

"How did you become a functional female? And what are these strangers from Gliid, the gods returned to Niond? And where's Yaedh?"

Iroedh started to tell about the death of Yaedh when another priestess raced up the road in a chariot. Up the path her ueg toiled and out of sight around toward the rear of the temple. A few seconds later the priestess panted back around the corner.

"Ystalverdh!" she cried. "Tell the Master at once. Wythias is marching on Ledhwid, searching for two strangers of another race."

"That must be the pair just arrived," said Ystalverdh, "whom Yaedh was sent to fetch. Oh, Garnedh!"

The other guard was already approaching. When the newly arrived priestess had given her message, Garnedh said:

"The Master says for the two Avtini to come in also."

"One surprise after another!" said Ystalverdh. "It *never* lets common visitors see its face. But go on—go on."

Garnedh led the way into an anteroom, then into the temple, with golden statues of the old gods around the sides and a smoking altar in the middle. Thence she conducted them through a curtained portal on the far side. As she neared the curtain Iroedh's nose caught the familiar scent of Bloch's pipe-tobacco.

The air in the chamber was stiflingly hot. Bloch sat on a cushion on the floor with his back to the portal, and at the sound of footsteps rose to his feet. Barbe remained upon her cushion, as did the third occupant of the room.

The third occupant was a roly-poly creature which if it had stood up would have come waist-high. It was covered all over with grizzled fur, and twiddled all fourteen digits of its seven-fingered hands. Iroedh would have thought it a mere pet had she not known it must be the Oracle.

The Oracle said, in fluent Avtinyk delivered in a high

squeaky voice: "Come in and make yourselves comfortable, Iroedh and Antis. You shouldn't have been held up outside had I known the whole story. What is it, Lhuidh?"

The priestess who had just arrived in the chariot gave her report.

When she had finished, the Oracle said: "By Dhiis, nothing is ever simple! Here I've promised myself another sight of my native world, and this complication comes up. I get along with most drone bands well enough, but this Wythias is impossible."

He gave the two priestesses a rapid series of orders to put the temple in condition for defense and to round up all the other priestesses in the neighborhood. During this harangue Bloch showed increasing signs of agitation and finally burst out:

"Gildakk, old man, don't you think it would be better to run for it? With a few hours' start we could lose ourselves in these hills——"

"And have them track us down in the open, when we have here one of the best natural defenses this side of Tvaar? Anyway, I'm too old and fat for racing up and down hills. We have a good stout wall and supplies for a long siege; my only worry is that I may not be able to round up more than twenty or thirty of my sisters. The rest are away on missions, but your guns should make up the difference."

Bloch said: "I have only about seventy rounds left, counting the pistol."

The Oracle twiddled its many fingers. "I should have liked more, but if you make every one count we may be able to hold them."

Antis said: "Why not get out the temple's chariots, head for Gliid, and shoot our way through the host?"

"Oh no!" cried Bloch, paling. "They'd block the road, or ambush us in the Gorge of Hwead and roll down rocks——"

"I fear my Terran colleague is right," said Gildakk, "considering my own age and infirmity, though if conditions were a little more favorable I'd chance it."

"Excuse me," said Iroedh.

"To be sure, you don't know me. My name is Gildakk, from the planet Thoth in the Procyonic system. I had just started to tell these Terrans how I became Oracle. When the party from my ship was held up by the road block, I drove right over it, but the next in line stopped and the rogues got the lot. When I arrived here I saw that the building was a public structure of some sort, so I hitched

125

my ueg out of sight and hung around a couple of days, nearly starved, until I found what was going on. Then I walked up to the guard and demanded to see the high priest or whatever they had inside. I figured it was an even chance whether they sacrificed me to some god or made a god of me."

"Thothians," Bloch put in, "are notoriously the worst gamblers in the Galaxy."

"Thank you. As it happened, the Oracle was a neuter-male named Enroys who'd been stolen as a child by the Arsuuni of Denüp and reared on a meatless diet as a slave. He'd escaped to Ledhwid, become an assistant to the previous Oracle, and taken the latter's place when she died.

"As for me, since I spoke no Avtinyk, the guards took me for somebody's pet. When I could get nothing from them save a pat on the head, I went back to my chariot. As it happened, my vehicle carried the party's load of signal pyrotechnics and little else. So I fetched a mine back up the hill, set it in front of the temple, and touched it off. The noise and the colored lights scared the wits out of the guards, and by the time they stopped running I was inside talking sign-language with Enroys. In due course I became his assistant and succeeded him. And I've put the Oracle on a business basis. I've made the priestesses into the best spy corps you ever saw, and I've filed and cross-indexed the prophecies properly. You should have seen them! All mixed up and written on leaves and potsherds and things."

Bloch, who had been looking around uneasily, said: "Shouldn't we—ah——"

"No, no, I've already done what needs doing. Unless that helicopter of yours shows up, in which case we'll use it."

Bloch said: "I have about given Kang up. I've watched for him every day, and I have a signal mirror, but no sign of him. Maybe he's crashed, or maybe they've given us up, or maybe they've flown away without us."

"Winston!" cried Barbe. "What a horrible idea!"

"Cheer up," said Gildakk. "If that's so, you may have to run the Oracle after I die. Since there's a pair of you, you won't find it so lonesome as I have. I admit I should like to see the gray seas of Thoth again. This insipid weather bores me."

"You should see its planet," said Bloch to Iroedh. "Practically one continuous hurricane. That's why it has all those fingers, to keep from being blown away."

"Excuse me, Gildakk," said Iroedh, "but are you a he or a she?"

"Both."

"You mean a neuter worker?"

"No; I'm a functional male and female at the same time. I both beget and bear—that is, when there's another Thothian to share the task. We are viviparous but not mammalian. Bloch was telling me about your metamorphosis, by the way. Enroys also discovered a meat diet, but too late in life to do him any good. He never did develop, poor fellow."

"Is it true that Wythias feeds his band on a mixed diet?"

"That's a secret I was holding out to make him behave, but yes, he does. He had ideas of conquering the planet that way, but now he knows of Bloch's guns I suppose he thinks that would be even quicker——" Gildakk snapped several fingers at once. "That gives me an idea! Instead of sitting here while Wythias besieges us, why not take the offensive?"

"How?" said Antis eagerly.

"If we could use Iroedh here, and some of the prophecies I have on file—if we could use them right we might take Wythias's band away from him. Then you could march through Avtinid knocking queens off their little thrones and setting up bisexual Communities——"

Iroedh protested: "But I don't want to be a conqueror! I just wish to settle down with Antis and lay his eggs and collect antiques! If anybody wishes to join us voluntarily——"

"You haven't much choice," said Gildakk. "It's the only way to beat Wythias, and then you'll find that who rides the noag cannot dismount. Besides, it will enable your race to resume their progress in the civilized arts."

"There is that, but——"

"Of course," said the Thothian. "All this fuss about sex seems silly to me, who am a whole complete individual and not a mere half-person like you one-sex beings; but I'm trying to be helpful. Here, let's see which pronouncement would work best . . ."

The Thothian rolled to its feet and limped over to a set of drawers. It pulled one out and began fingering through a file of bark cards, humming to itself.

"Here's one," it said:

"The High Queen rides in a chariot bright
With a Princess Royal between the shafts,

While the Arsuuny soldiers in panic flight
Abandon their rafts."

"What does it mean?" asked Iroedh, looking over Gildakk's shoulder.

"Oh, it doesn't *mean* anything! Or, rather, it means whatever the hearer wishes it to mean. I issued that one a few years ago to the envoys from Yeym, when the Arsuuni were attacking that Community."

"But Yeym was destroyed!"

"Of course it was; but I saw no harm in encouraging the poor things when they were fighting for their lives."

"Why rafts?"

"Because it rhymes and fits the meter. Here's another:

> *"When the Rogue Queen wears a crown of light*
> *The Golden Couch shall be overthrown;*
> *When the gods descend from heaven's height*
> *Shall the seed be sown.*

"See? You're the rogue queen; the golden couch is the present sex-caste system with its oversexed queens and neuter workers; Bloch and the other Terrans are the gods; and the seed is that of these drones we're trying to win over. It couldn't be better if I had composed it specially for the occasion. Of course I've already applied it to other events a couple of times, but nobody will remember that."

Iroedh asked: "How about the crown of light?"

"Hmm, crown of light, crown of light. Garnedh! Get one of the sisters to help you drag Chest Number Four from the cellar, will you?"

Iroedh said: "Then it's all just an imposture? There's no real prophetic knowledge? The Oracle doesn't go into a mystic trance and interpret the sound of the bells?"

"Of course it's a fake! Since I hope to leave here soon, I have no reason to deceive you. The sooner you and Antis learn to rely upon yourselves alone, and not on any of this mummery, the better off you'll be. Ah, thank you, sisters. Now. let's see . . ."

Gildakk opened the chest, in which lay a litter of unfamiliar-looking tubular objects.

"Signal flares," he said. "I hope they haven't deteriorated too much in all these years."

X. The Temple Grove

Toward evening, looking south from the portico of the temple, Iroedh saw dust rising from the Gorge of Hwead. Preparations for defense speeded up. From the temple came the sounds of a grindstone sharpening spearheads, and a general hammering and sawing mingled with the ever-present sound of the bells of Ledhwid.

Some of the priestesses had piled logs on the slope just above the gate, behind a pair of stakes driven into the ground, so that if the stakes were removed the logs would roll down and pile up in a heap against the inner side of the gate to lend it additional strength. Others stacked arrows and spears, or erected wicker mantlets to protect the defenders against arrow fire. For the twentieth time Iroedh felt the edge of her machete. It was as sharp as whetting could make it, and with the handsome armor provided by the temple she should make an effective warrior.

Still, there was no blinking the fact that Gildakk had been able to round up only eighteen priestesses, of which two or three were too old to be of real use in fighting. With the addition of her party, therefore, they had at most twenty effectives. No doubt the Terrans' gunfire would account for the first attackers and discourage the rest, but if Wythias pushed his attack regardless of losses . . .

It seemed to Iroedh that of the three alternatives they had discussed—to flee, to shoot their way through the host, or to stand their ground—they had chosen the worst. Why hadn't she put up an argument? She had become so wrapped up in her love for Antis that she was getting into the habit of blindly following his lead.

The band of Wythias was now in sight, crawling up the road from the gorge like creeping things after a sweet. As they came nearer, Iroedh's dilating pupils could see several ueg chariots at the head of the column. No doubt they were those the band had stolen from Bloch's party.

The drones came nearer and nearer, then spread out

129

around the base of the Hill of Ledhwid like a trickle of water that meets an obstacle. A trumpet sounded back in the temple, and Iroedh went to her assigned place near the gate.

A drone in full panoply marched up the path to the gate, threw back his head, and bawled: "O Oracle!"

"Yes?" squeaked Gildakk, peering beadily over the gate with a shawl around his head.

"Are you indeed the Oracle of Ledhwid?" asked the herald, eyes bulging.

"Absolutely. Don't you remember the prophecy:

> *"When knaves to Ledhwid Temple shall come*
> *With impious hands to plunder her,*
> *They'll be scattered like chaff by an Oracle small*
> *And covered with fur"*?

"I did not know that one," said the herald. "But to get down to business: Our leader demands that you give up to him the people from the sky ship who have taken refuge with you, together with their magical weapons."

"What people?"

"There's no use lying, Oracle. A worker of Khwiem passed them on the road this morning, and told us about it before we slew her; and a scout we left to watch the Gorge of Hwead told us a party answering the same description passed through the gorge around noon and entered the temple grounds. So render them up or take the consequences."

"How am I supposed to do that?"

"How do you mean?"

"These strangers have godlike powers. They can blast you with lightning and thunder as easily as they can look at you."

"We know."

"Then how shall I coerce them, even if I were willing?"

"That's your problem," said the herald.

"Then you will have to catch them yourselves. I can do nothing."

"Will you and your people leave the temple grounds while we come in after the sky folk?"

Iroedh had a bad moment; it would be easy for Gildakk to sell them out in exchange for his personal safety.

"No," said the Thothian. "This sacred enclosure shall not be profaned by armed invasion."

"Then you and yours shall perish, I warn you."

130

"Wait, herald," said Gildakk. "If Wythias would care to parley, I have a counteroffer——"

"No proposals! My leader knows how clever you are and will not be drawn into negotiations. You shall either give us the fugitives, or get out of the way while we get them."

"We defy you. Your leader shall find that trying to take this place with a mob of brigands is like a new-hatched babe trying to crack a dairtel nut with its gums."

The herald went away. Those in the enclosure braced themselves.

The red sun sank below the ridges. Iroedh knew now that there was no hope of help from the *Paris,* for Bloch had assured her that it was against the Terrans' policy to try to land the helicopter in strange places at night.

Though there were over two hundred drones in the band, they had to spread themselves out in a pretty thin line to surround the Hill of Ledhwid. At the sound of the trumpet they started forward. When some of them broke into a run their officers called them back. As the rogues came closer and their circle contracted, their line became denser, though at the base of the hill there was still some arms' lengths between individuals. Up they came, first walking, then half crawling as the slope became steeper.

The trumpet sounded from the temple. Priestesses picked up great round stones from the poles behind the wall and heaved them over.

"Iroedh, throw your stones!" said a voice behind her.

Iroedh pulled herself together and hurled a stone as big as her head. It ricocheted down the slope, bounding clear over the head of an advancing drone. A second flew between two of them. Crash! One had struck a drone off to Iroedh's right. As the attacker's body rolled back down the slope, other drones stopped to watch. The line became disordered. Another drone went down under the bombardment. The officers ordered the line forward; some obeyed.

In front of Iroedh a little group of rogues struggled up the slope. She poised a stone and hurled it. Two spear lengths' away they paused and looked as the stone came at them, then flinched aside. The stone struck with a smack into the midst of them; there were bodies flying and bodies rolling and bodies running. When the confusion abated one drone lay still on the slope, another dragged himself along the ground, and the rest ran back down to the base of the hill.

The drones' trumpet sounded recall. The rest of the drones ran back down the slope in great bounds.

"How's it going, Iroedh?" said Bloch behind her. He was prowling up and down with the gun under his arm.

"Have we won?"

"Not by a jugful! They'll be back. I wish they had got close enough to warrant shooting; the gun becomes less effective as it gets darker, in spite of this infrared viewer. I wish I had your night vision."

"This wall doesn't look like much protection."

Bloch shook his head. "In most places it's only breast-high; they can boost each other over it. Gildakk tells me the builders never meant it for a defense, but merely to keep wild animals out of the grove and the tame animals in."

The rogues' trumpet sounded again, this time to call them together. They formed a solid black mass on the plain below, the mutter of their leaders' instructions wafting up to Iroedh at her post.

They organized themselves into a rectangular phalanx and, at another trumpet blast, headed up the slope toward the gate, all two hundred of them. Those behind the front rank held their shields over their heads so that the mass looked like a scale-backed creeping thing.

Iroedh called: "Daktablak! Bring your gun! The rest of you fetch more stones!"

The scaly monster swept up the slope, slower as it became steeper. Inside the enclosure priestesses grunted as they staggered along the wall with stones in their arms.

Then the stones began to fall again. One bounded over the entire testudo; others clanged against the shields. A few drones went down, but the rest closed up and came on. Some priestesses began shooting arrows into the mass. A great stone crashed into the front rank and its impact swept a whole file of drones sprawling, but the others untangled themselves and struggled on.

"Daktablak!" cried Iroedh. "They'll gain the wall!"

She hurled a last stone and reached for her machete. Then the gun went off deafeningly: *bang-bang-bang,* shooting out bright orange flashes into the dusk. The drone advance came to a halt, then the whole mass dissolved into its component drones running for safety.

Bloch, putting another clip into the gun, said: "I can kill two or three with one shot when they're bunched like that. How many did I get?"

"There are over twenty lying there, but I don't know how many are yours," said Iroedh. "Where's Antis?"

"On the other side of the grove. It would surprise me if

Wythias can drive his people to another attack." Bloch filled and lit his pipe.

The rogues had called another conference on the plain. Voices could be heard, raised in loud debate. After a long wait they got into motion again. They trickled off around both sides of the hill, as on the first attack. This time, however, instead of forming a single line, they organized themselves into a dozen or more small groups. At the signal these came bounding up the slope with almost as much *élan* as the first time.

"Bless my soul!" said Bloch. "Those fellows have nerve, to come back after the last strafing. Not many Terran primitives would do that."

"Perhaps they're more afraid of Wythias than of you," grunted Iroedh, lifting a stone to hurl.

In the fading light it was hard to tell how effective the missiles were. From elsewhere on the perimeter came the cry:

"Daktablak! Daktablak! Come quickly!"

Iroedh had a glimpse of Bloch's bald head bobbing away toward the sound; then in a few seconds came the crash of the rifle. Then from another section of the wall:

"Daktablak! Come!"

From Iroedh's left there came the clash and grind of weapons. She looked along the wall toward a dark knot of struggling figures, drew her machete, and started toward them. Before she arrived she heard the high voice of Barbe:

"Stand back, you stupids!"

The group opened out and the little Terran figure stepped into the opening. Her pistol cracked several times, and the rogues who had gained the inside of the wall slumped to the ground.

A priestess looking toward Iroedh cried: "Look out!"

Iroedh turned to see the head of a drone rising over the wall beside her. She whirled and struck backhand at the neck; felt the blade bite. The head toppled out of sight and the spouting torso followed it. Somewhere across the enclosure the big gun was firing again, and among the giant trees a drone who had gained the enclosure fought priestesses. Iroedh started toward the sound, but by the time she arrived the drone was down.

Then all noises ceased save the footsteps of running drones. Bloch and Antis appeared, the former doing things to his gun and the latter wiping a slight wound on his cheek. Bloch said:

"I hope that's the last. While we've only suffered three

or four casualties, we have a total of six rounds left for the rifle and two for the pistol. We're even running low on stones."

The rogues slowly gathered themselves together again upon the plain. Antis said:

"Wythias must have lost a fifth of his band. He can't do this many times more."

"Once more is all that will be required," said Bloch gloomily. "Why did I ever go in for xenological exploration? I should have stayed home and been a professor."

Below, argument raged again among the assembled drones. Injured rogues dragged themselves from where they had fallen toward the main mass. Some of the drones lit campfires and torches.

At last one rogue mounted the path to the gate, holding a torch over his head. Iroedh recognized the herald, who called:

"O Oracle!"

"Had enough?" squealed Gildakk from the wall.

"We have not given up, if that is what you mean. Though you defy our direct assault, we can still starve you out."

"That will take a long time."

"We can wait. However, as all of us have other business, my leader generously offers you a parley, to see what proposal you could possibly make that would interest him as much as getting the sky peoples' weapons."

"Very well," said the Thothian. "On my side there will be myself, the sky folk, and the two who came with them. Wythias may bring not more than four officers with him, unarmed, and must stand two spears' lengths below us. We shall stand just outside the gate."

"We don't care about the Avtini; leave them out of it."

"No; the proposal concerns them."

"Very well, bring them. But your party must also be unarmed; especially the sky folk must not have their magical weapons."

"We agree," said Gildakk. "And since the proposal also concerns your band as a whole, it is only proper that they should hear. Let them gather with torches on the slope below Wythias, but not closer than three spears' lengths from him . . ."

After some more dickering about distances, to guard against treachery, the herald agreed and departed. Gildakk said to Iroedh:

"Quick, take off your armor and tunic and put on your cloak!"

134

When the drones had gathered upon the slope with torches fluttering, and the logs had been dragged away from the inner side of the gate, Iroedh filed out of the gate with the others: Gildakk, Bloch, Barbe, and Antis. Iroedh, wrapped in her cloak, felt qualms at leaving her machete inside the wall and had to control a tendency to glance back at the gate every few seconds to make sure it still stood open. Antis was likewise unarmed, and Bloch and Barbe held up their hands to show they were empty. Barbe had even left her pistol holster behind.

A pair of priestesses carried lighted oil lamps out through the gate and set them on the path to provide additional illumination. Iroedh looked into the torchlit confusion below. A little group of drones, muffled in their cloaks, was ascending the hill. In front came one huge drone whose matted crest rose above a pair of fierce eyes.

Gildakk, standing beside Antis, said: "Ask which is Wythias." It had been arranged that Antis, having the loudest voice, should do the talking.

"I am Wythias," said the giant. "Speak."

At least, thought Iroedh, it was lucky the drones used only bows and spears, for neither could readily be hidden under a cloak.

Gildakk squeaked to Antis, phrase by phrase, and Antis repeated the phrases in his piercing bellow. This gave the speech a somewhat jerky effect, though Iroedh found it all the more impressive for its pauses.

"Wythias, officers, and men of the band of Wythias!" began Gildakk and Antis. "You think you wish the magical weapons of the sky people to conquer the world, do you not?"

"Yes!" replied Wythias, and this was echoed by several of his drones.

"But that is not what you really desire. You may think you lead a good life; you have food and drink and games and ornaments and excitement. But there is one thing you do *not* have. You know what I mean?"

"Yes!" roared the drones.

Wythias said: "What do you expect to do? Provide us each with a queen, or some such fantastic idea?"

"Not fantastic, my dear Wythias. If you listen to us, every one of you can have—not some fat old queen who bosses you and whom you share with sixteen other drones —but a handsome and congenial functional female of your own. Your very own! To love and live with all your life, as the ancients used to do. Who will lay your eggs, which

135

will hatch into children that you, and you alone, may rear up as you wish. What do you think of *that?*"

A murmur went through the drones. Wythias said: "A likely story! Next you'll offer us the Treasure of Inimdhad. Where is your proof?"

"I have proof. Iroedh, show them."

Iroedh stepped forward, threw off her cloak, and stood naked before them in the torchlight.

"There!" continued Antis-Gildakk. "A perfect functional female, once a neuter like all workers. I can change workers into functional females!"

A drone stood up. "How do we know she's been changed? How do we know she's not merely some runaway princess?"

"Is there any drone here from Elham?"

"I am," said a voice.

"Dyos, you scoundrel!" roared Antis. "You knew Iroedh of Elham, who hauled you out of the prison cell, didn't you?"

"Y-yes."

"Then step forward and identify her."

Dyos came up hesitantly, looked, and said: "That's Iroedh. Just a minute to make sure those things aren't glued on . . ."

"Ouch!" said Iroedh. "You——"

"Yes, she's turned functional. It's true, fellows."

"But," said Wythias, "how do we know workers would accept this arrangement, assuming you transformed them?"

"Iroedh did. She is united to Antis by such a contract now, aren't you, Iroedh?"

"Yes," said Iroedh, "and I love it."

"Of course," continued Antis and Gildakk, "there will have to be some changes. If you go ahead with this project you must accept our leadership; you will have to stop killing workers. Every worker, remember, is a potential female! Waste not, want not. You must——"

"Ridiculous!" shouted Wythias. "I won't give up my leadership to anybody! And this is all a hoax of some kind to get these sky folk out of my hands, and we shall be left holding an empty sack."

"I'm not finished, please!" Antis and Gildakk went on to rhapsodize on the beauties of married life, then said:

"But most of all we urge you to join us because this revolution was foretold long ago by the divine prescience of the never-failing Oracle of Ledhwid. In the incumbency of my predecessor Enroys, of sacred memory, the divine afflatus issued the following promise:

> *"When the Rogue Queen wears a crown of light*
> *The Golden Couch shall be overthrown;*
> *When the gods descend from heaven's height*
> *Shall the seed be sown.*

Which is interpreted as follows: The Rogue Queen is obviously Iroedh. The Golden Couch is the present sex-caste system with its queens. The sky folk are the gods; the seed is yours. And as for the crown of light——"

Gildakk squeaked over his shoulder: "Light up!"

There were faint noises from inside the wall and a whisper: "The first one won't light!"

"Then try the next!"

The audience squirmed and rustled at the length of the pause.

"As for the crown of light——" repeated Antis.

Then it came: a sputter, a flare, a loud foomp, something soaring into the sky, a sharp pop, and a blinding magenta light drifting slowly overhead in the evening air. Then another went off, soared, exploded in a dazzling spray of green sparks, and finished with a vivid flash and an ear-shattering *bang*.

"There you are," said Antis. "Down with Queen Danoakor's so-called reforms! Back to the happy customs of the Golden Age! Let's overturn the Golden Couch, as prophesied by the Oracle!"

The fireworks had brought cries of astonishment and alarm from the drones. One shouted:

"It's the fire-breathing Igog!"

At the last explosion many near the edges of the crowd had started to run away. Gildakk said:

"Your music, quickly!"

Antis put the flute to his lips, and Iroedh joined Bloch and Barbe in singing the Terran song: *"Main aidh av siin dhe glory . . ."*

The audience calmed down, and those who had started to flee wandered back. A drone called:

"I know you, Antis! You're no drone but the god Dhiis come back to Niond. I know you by that ancient instrument you play!"

Gildakk and Antis concluded: "Who's with us? Who wants to try it?"

Iroedh, somewhat shaken by the pyrotechnics, could see

the faces of the rogues turning and hear the murmur of voices. One drone raised his hand:

"Count me in!" "And me!" "And me!" "*Kwa* Queen Iroedh!"

Hands rose all over the assemblage. Wythias glaring, shouted:

"It's a trick! A cowardly, treacherous, dastardly, stinking trick! You call a parley and instead make lying speeches and sing songs to turn my own men against me!"

"Not at all; you'd be just as welcome as———"

"I'll stop your lies about every worker a queen and a queen for every drone!"

Wythias threw back his cloak, revealing that in one hand he held a spear cut to half length so that it could be hidden. His arm darted back, then forward. The spear whizzed up the slope.

Iroedh, with a little shriek, reached for the machete that was not there. Out of the corner of her eye she saw Barbe's hand dart inside her shirt.

The spear struck Gildakk in the belly and went on until the point, now green with Thothian blood, came out its back. Barbe's hand reappeared with her pistol. Gildakk fell backwards, twitching. The pistol barked and spat a sheet of flame: once, twice.

Wythias staggered back a step, then folded slowly into a heap.

While Iroedh braced herself to spring for the gate, Barbe, holding the pistol steady, called in a high voice: "Don't start anything, any of you! You have all seen that treacherous murder. Calm yourselves, my littles, and give consideration to your situation. Your bad leader, he is gone and our offer is still open. Join us and forget the unhappy past. As the Oracle told you, the change is bound to come. Will you work with it or be crushed by it? If you wish time to consider———"

"I have considered," said a drone. "I'm with you."

"So am I," said another. "Wythias would have had us all killed to further his ambitions."

The others joined in assent, all but a very few who straggled off into the night. Iroedh heard Barbe murmur to Bloch:

"Hold me up, Winston darling. I think I'm going to faint. Those were my last bullets."

"Really, Barbe," said Bloch, "you shouldn't have brought that gun. We promised———"

"Oh, what stupidity! He had the spear, didn't he?"

Iroedh leaned over Gildakk. The Thothian's beady eyes looked up at her and its voice squeaked faintly.

"Iroedh!"

"Yes? What can I do for you?"

"Nothing; I'm finished. I wanted to see the gray seas again, but no such luck. I have one piece of advice."

"Yes?"

"If your revolution breaks down the—present Community pattern, revive the old religion."

"Why? I don't really believe in it, and I'm sure you don't."

"Without the present Communities—the Avtini will need—an emotional outlet—to take their place. And a unifying force—so you can fight the Arsuuni—and . . ."

The voice trailed off and the bright eyes closed. Gildakk the Thothian was dead.

XI. The Battle

Next morning Kang dropped out of the sky in his helicopter. "Was up on practice flight last night," he said. "Saw flares."

He went on to explain in his truncated English that he had had a slight accident, bending the alighting gear of the machine, so that it had been laid up for several days. Then it was grounded further by bad weather, and when he finally took off to search for the party (lack of radio reports from whom had aroused alarm on the *Paris*) he could find no sign of them along the road to Ledhwid. A well-armed ground party was now searching for them.

Bloch told Antis and Iroedh: "Well, this is nearly the end of the road for us, though for you it's just a beginning. What are you going to do next?"

Iroedh looked with some consternation at Antis, who returned her stare. It struck her for the first time that she would soon no longer have these wise and potent Terrans to rely on. As Gildakk had said, she and Antis would have to learn to depend upon themselves, no matter how puzzling or perilous their course.

She said: "I suppose we shall get in touch with the other rogue drone bands and try to persuade them to join us. Then we'll start a campaign to win over the neighboring Communities, either as wholes or by seducing away individual workers."

Bloch suggested: "You might write messages, wrap them around arrows, and shoot them over the walls."

"Splendid! And then we shall—— But who is that approaching?"

A chariot was smoking up the road from the Gorge of Hwead. As it came closer Iroedh saw that it was driven by a priestess of the Oracle. As the driver neared, she pulled in her ueg at the sight of the drones encamped upon the plain and started to turn her vehicle around.

Iroedh, calling reassurance, ran toward the chariot. The driver hesitated on the verge of flight until Iroedh came up and tried to brief her on the situation in one short sentence.

"But where," said the priestess, "is our Master?"

"Dead. Wythias killed it and then was slain himself."

"Great Eunmar! Whom then did it choose as successor?"

"Nobody; it had no time. Won't you come in?"

"If I can do so safely. Wythias's drones kill on sight."

"No more. You can see some of your fellow priestesses moving among them unmolested."

The priestess came timorously, saying: "I have important news for the Master, but since he's dead I don't know whom to give it to."

"Tell me, why don't you? Since I find myself in a somewhat authoritative position around here——"

"Oh, it wouldn't interest you, Queen. The Arsuuni of Tvaarm have routed the advanced force of the Elhamni and are now invading Elham's territory——"

"*What?* Oh, Antis!"

"Yes?" When told the news Antis looked shaken, then put on his firm face. "So what? What did they ever do for us except try to kill us and drive us out? Let the Arsuuni have them."

"Antis, think! We shall have to face the problem of the Arsuuni. If we don't destroy them they'll exterminate us sooner or later. Our only hope is to unite all the Communities, or whatever takes the place of the Communities under the new system, to crush the Arsuuny Communities one by one. And how can we start better than with our own? If we let it be destroyed we shall not only lose part

140

of our eventual force, but others will say: They care only for their own power, so why should we trust them?"

"Hmmp," said Antis. "I'll think it over——"

"Not this time," said Iroedh, knowing that meant that he would come out with the suggestion as his own idea the following day. "Every day is vital."

"What do you propose?"

"Go to Elham myself and put the case to them: If they wish to survive, join forces with your drones to fight the Arsuuni."

"They'd kill you before you could open your mouth."

"You forget I'm now a queen!" Iroedh proudly threw out her breasts. "A functional female may not be attacked by a worker under any circumstances, but only by another functional female. When Queen Rhuar went mad and began killing the workers of Elham, and they had no princess of age to send against her, not even then did they harm her. They seized her with bare hands (though several died in the doing), carried her gently outside the walls, and left her."

"What happened to her?"

"They found her remains half eaten, though whether the beasts slew her or whether she died first of starvation they never learned."

"It sounds good, but you can't go yet."

"Why not?"

"Because it will take me days to get my people organized, and there's no sense in your getting to Elham much ahead of me. The Arsuuni might kill you. When you walk into that gate I want to be close behind with my drones."

No argument would shake Antis from that resolution, though he finally admitted with a shamefaced grin: "To tell the truth, my reasons aren't entirely tactical."

"What then?"

"If you must know, I can't bear to be separated from you longer than necessary, do you see?"

"Why, Antis! To put your petty personal feelings ahead of the future of the race——"

"Don't sneer at personal feelings. It was because of them that you rescued me from the cell and started all these events!"

When told of their plans, Bloch said: "Don't be surprised to find me breathing down your neck from the helicopter, especially if there's a battle. Subbarau would postpone his flying date a week for some good action movies."

"Wouldn't you help us?"

"No. Sorry, but I've explained that. Ready, Barbe?"

Barbe kissed Iroedh, shook the hand of Antis (who seemed puzzled by the gesture), and climbed into the helicopter. They smiled, waved, and rose.

A rogue drone, leaning on his spear, remarked: "They *are* the gods! I shall tell my offspring, if I ever have any, how I saw them with my own eyes."

Nearly two eight-days later, Iroedh and her escort approached Elham. Although she had promised Antis not to get too far ahead of his army, she could not help speeding up a little as she neared her Community. She more than half expected to find it laid waste by the Arsuuni, though when she passed the *Paris* at Gliid her friends there assured her that they had not heard of any such catastrophe.

Bloch told her surreptitiously: "I shouldn't say this because it might be deemed intervention, but I flew over your city yesterday on a visit to Khinam and saw no sign of the enemy."

She continued on her way, bearing the Terrans' assurances of moral if not material support. Iroedh thought moral support all very nice, but she would much have preferred the loan of a gun.

As she drove, the leader of the escort, a former officer of Wythias named Tregaros, waxed garrulous about the fights he had been in:

". . . now, Queen, see that crag? Well, one time when Wythias sent us through here to pick up an order of spearheads from Umwys the smith, the Thidhemni tried to ambush us. But I had a point out, as Wythias taught me. Eh, he was a tyrant, old Wythias, but as smart a soldier as you'll find the length and breadth of Avtinid. And I also remembered the prophecy:

> *"When the noag for prey shall lie in wait*
> *And leap for the leipag with golden eyes,*
> *The leipag shall with a vakhnag mate*
> *As the noag dies.*

So when I saw that crag I said to myself, Tregaros, wouldn't that be a fine place for an ambush? Slow down, boys; we want to look into this. And, sure enough, up the road came the point, beating his beast for all he was worth, with the Thidhemni after him. The sil v creatures hadn't had the sense to let him go through and 'ttack our main body. So we ambushed them instead of the other way round."

Iroedh tried dutifully to listen, but found her mind wandering off into fantasies of her hoped-for reunion with Antis. She knew what he would want first.

At the frontier of Elham the guards of Queen Maiur and Queen Estir all stared as the party drew up. The Thidhemny guard said:

"We got word to let you through, though why we cannot understand. So pass on."

Iroedh could have told her the reason was an ultimatum from Antis, informing Queen Maiur's government that he proposed to pass through the territory of Thidhem in full force, and *if* not hindered would restrain his drones from doing harm. The guards on the other side were even more nonplused when Iroedh said:

"I am Queen Iroedh, on my way for a formal visit to Elham, and these drones are my escort."

"Are you the Iroedh who used to be a worker of Elham?"

"That is right."

"Great Eunmar! I didn't know you with those bulges!"

"I'm glad you do now. How's the Community making out under Estir?"

The Elhamni looked at one another, evidently uncertain whether to discuss intramural matters with one who had become an outsider. One of the Thidhemni spoke:

"Oh, they're having a terrible time. Estir has proved more difficult and domineering even than our own Maiur. We had the Queens' Conference at Thidhem last eight-day, you know, and instead of behaving with such modesty as becomes a new queen, and trying to learn something of her business from the older ones, Estir spent her time telling them how to reign, as if they hadn't been doing so for years. She practically insulted the Queen of Hawardem, and you can be sure they crossed Estir off their social lists in a hurry."

One of the Elhamny guards spoke up: "Since you will find out anyway, Iroedh, I'll admit they're right. Estir has been a trial. And many of us sympathized with you over your expulsion. Not that we don't think you were at fault too, but Estir tried to deal treacherously with you. And a queen's honor is that of her Community."

The other said: "It doesn't matter, with the Arsuuni coming down upon us any day. Did I hear you name yourself queen?"

"So you did."

"But how—what are you queen *of?*"

"Of King Antis, if you must know."

143

"How is that possible? Antis was a drone of Elham who escaped a Cleanup; unless this is another of the same name. And 'king' is an obsolete term——"

"I haven't time to explain, sisters, and I think you had better let us through. Don't be alarmed when a whole army of drones appears behind me."

The outnumbered guards dubiously let Iroedh and her drones pass. They drove over the Lhanwaed Hills, along the beach of the Scarlet Sea, past Khinad Point, and up the main highway to Elham itself. Iroedh felt an odd lump in her throat as the well-remembered wall and domes materialized out of the trees. Still, she wished that Antis were with her; whatever his faults, lack of courage was not among them. She told Tregaros:

"Wait here out of sight of the main gate. In case of trouble, try to get word to Antis."

She drove on. As soon as she came in sight of the fields there was a running about of the double guards posted there. The alarm of the workers subsided when they saw it was not the Arsuuni but only a single Avtin in a chariot.

At the main gate Iroedh received an argument like that at the frontier, with much the same result. While one guard ran ahead to inform the officers, others escorted Iroedh in.

When she drove up to the main portal of the Community, workers were gathering from all parts of the complex. The crowd buzzed excitedly as it opened to let Iroedh pass. On the front steps the officers of the Council were gathering with their insignia around their necks. From the crowd came the harsh voice of Rhodh:

"It is Iroedh the traitor! I always knew she would come to a shameful end!"

Rhodh had evidently not changed. Iroedh held up a hand and began:

"Greetings, workers of Elham. Know that I am Queen Iroedh, whom you formerly knew as Worker Iroedh, the mate of King Antis, formerly Drone Antis. We rule, not a patch of land, but an army of stout-hearted and strong-muscled drones, formerly rogue drones——"

"Why aren't they still rogues?" asked the general.

"Because we are starting them on a new way of life. To make you understand I shall have to tell you some personal history . . ."

Iroedh had started to narrate the story of her introduction to a meat diet when there was another stir in the crowd and Queen Estir burst through, wearing by her side the original steel machete that Iroedh had stolen from the Terrans.

"What's this?" she cried. "Another queen in my Community? She shan't live ten seconds——"

"Please, Queen, let her finish," said the foreign officer. "This is important."

Iroedh resumed her story, including her union with Antis. The foreign officer interrupted:

"What, specifically, do you propose?"

"First, to form an alliance between Elham and my army against the Arsuuni. For one thing we can furnish you all with matselhi, which for close combat are more effective——"

"Never!" cried Estir. "I have declared the matselh a royal weapon, to be used by none but queens!"

"I don't think we want newfangled things like that anyway," said the general. "The spear has stood us in good stead since time immemorial, and that thing of yours looks like an uncivilized and inhumane weapon. But go on."

"Then, assuming we can defeat the Arsuuni, those of you who wish to join us, become functional females, and mate with our drones may do so."

"But, Queen Iroedh," began the agricultural officer, "what will happen if——"

"Queen Iroedh!" shrieked Estir. "You are Iroedh, the runaway worker! The one who delivered the condemned drones from their cell!"

"Yes, as I was explaining when——"

"You mean you not only dare invade my Community without permission; you propose to seduce away my workers with your monstrous, perverted, unnatural proposal! To destroy the very basis of my society! If every worker became a queen, what distinction would there be to being a queen? Guards, slay me this revolting monstrosity at once!"

As some of the guards (among whom Iroedh recognized her old friend Vardh) raised their spears, Iroedh called: "Wait! After all, I'm a queen, and none of you may raise a hand against me!"

The guards drew back, exchanging baffled looks. Another ueg chariot came through the main gate at a run. The worker driving it leaped down from her vehicle before it had stopped and ran up.

"Queen Estir——"

"Quiet! I'm occupied."

"But——"

145

"I said quiet! Get out! Now then, guards, why don't you kill this obscene travesty of a queen? You heard me, didn't you?"

"Yes, Queen, but she *is* a functional female," said one, "and the basic law says—"

"Then I'll show you!" screeched Estir, drawing her machete and rushing toward Iroedh's chariot.

Iroedh had not counted upon a duel with Estir, having in fact forgotten all about the original machete until the sight of it on Estir's hip recalled it to her mind. Now she had no time to don armor. As she leaped down from the chariot her main thought was that Antis would be furious at her having run such a risk. She was not really afraid of Estir, who was also nude, for Iroedh's many days of roughing it and clearing trails had hardened her.

Clang! clang! went the blades as Estir struck overhand, forehand, and backhand. Iroedh parried and got in a cut of her own, which Estir knocked easily aside and struck again with lightning speed. Iroedh now remembered with a touch of horror what an exercise-fanatic Estir had been as princess. She must have kept herself in prime condition.

They circled, advancing, retreating, slashing, parrying, dodging, and feinting. Iroedh realized that the steel blade was much superior, being at once lighter, stronger, and sharper. Her own blade was acquiring visible bends and almost enough notches to make a saw out of it, while that of Estir seemed undamaged.

Iroedh tried to remember some of the things Bloch had told her about swords; how Terrans had once used them for thrusting . . . She shifted her grip to prepare for a thrust at Estir's advanced knee.

Then Estir struck Iroedh's blade with all her might. The machete flew out of Iroedh's tingling hand and fell on the greensward sixteen paces away.

"Now!" cried Estir, poising on the balls of her feet.

Iroedh knew she was finished. Estir could run like a streak, and if Iroedh turned to flee or to run for the machete, Estir would have the steel blade into her back before she had taken three steps.

Estir advanced, swinging the machete, poised for a dash. Iroedh backed, visualizing her head bouncing along the ground as poor Queen Intar's had done. Up came the blade as Estir leaped. The flash of sunlight on steel held Iroedh's gaze as in a vise. Poor Antis . . .

There was a heavy thud as a red-smeared bronze point appeared, projecting a hand's breadth from Estir's chest just below her right breast. Instead of completing her rush

146

upon Iroedh, Estir fell forward to hands and knees with a spear-shaft sticking out of her back like a mast. Her arms gave way beneath her and she crumpled to the gravel of the driveway. Blood ran from her mouth.

Iroedh looked to see who had thrown the spear. The workers were all backing away with exclamations of horror from one who stood in the armor of a guard but without her spear. Under the helmet Iroedh recognized Vardh.

"Vardh!" she exclaimed. "You saved my life."

The crowd continued to point and murmur: "She killed a queen!" "She killed a queen!" "Slay her!" "Burn her!" "Tear her to pieces!"

"You shall do nothing of the sort!" said Iroedh. "Let her alone, do you hear?"

Vardh said shakily: "I know it was wrong, Iroedh darling, but I still love you better than anyone, and I couldn't stand by while she killed you. *Weu!* Now I suppose I shall have to kill myself too."

"Nonsense! I suppose I am now Queen of Elham."

"Oh no!" said the general. "You didn't slay Estir in fair fight!"

"But I'm of pure Elhamny blood even if the duel wasn't fought according to regulations. . . . What is it?"

The worker who had driven up in the chariot had been trying to attract Iroedh's attention. This newcomer now said:

"Queen Iroedh, the Arsuuni are approaching! They surrounded the remains of the scouting force and slew them all so that only I escaped!"

"Good Gwyyr!" Iroedh looked around; a swarm of workers was pouring in through the main gate from the fields. She told the general:

"We'll argue the future of Elham later; you'd better get ready for battle."

While hundreds of workers ran madly about under the general's orders, Iroedh buckled on the armor she had been given at Ledhwid, walked down to the gate, and climbed one of the gate towers. She could not see Tregaros and his squad, and wondered if she should try to join him. On the other hand, he might already have left to seek Antis's army, and her desertion of the Community at this point would ruin her standing with them and lower their morale.

A noise caused her to look in the other direction, and there was the helicopter from the *Paris*, hovering over the spot where the road to the southeast ran through the

147

vremoel orchard. That would be Bloch with his picture-making machine. But what was that dust rising from the orchard? Sun flashed on brass, and Iroedh realized that Bloch, in his subtle way, was trying to help her by hovering squarely over the advancing Arsuuni.

Iroedh went back to the main portal and picked up the steel machete. She told the general about the approach of the enemy, and asked: "Where can I sharpen this? It's not——"

"But you cannot fight! You're a queen!"

"A minute ago you were saying I couldn't be queen of Elham!"

"You're still a functional female, and the workers insist that the decencies be preserved. Go to the royal dome and await the outcome of the battle."

"Ridiculous!" Iroedh marched off to hunt a grindstone for herself. She found one and stood in line while the workers ahead of her sharpened their spearheads.

An uproar from outside the wall drew her attention. Armored workers were running back and forth along the wall, and beyond them Iroedh could see the tops of dozens of scaling ladders placed against the wall by the Arsuuni, who were wasting no time in beginning their assault. Next among the little figures on the wall appeared the much bigger forms of Arsuuny soldiers, climbing up their ladders and trying to force their way over the wall. The workers who had been sharpening their weapons ran to take their places in the defense.

The Arsuuni had carried to its next logical step the sex-caste system imposed upon the Avtini by Queen Danoakor. In fact, before that the Arsuuni had been another race of the same species, little different from the Avtini. They had, however, found it possible through dietary control to produce not only a caste of neuter-female workers, but also a subcaste of neuter-female soldiers afflicted with a form of acromegalic giantism. Over a head taller than a normal worker, they impressed the Avtini, with their great knobby hands and huge jaws, as hideous monsters. In the Arsuuny hierarchy the queen was at the top; below her were the soldiers (who really ran the Community) and below them the workers, and below *them* the large body of Avtiny slaves who did most of the actual labor.

After a hasty sharpening of her blade, Iroedh ran after the workers to a point on the wall that seemed to be under heavy pressure. As she arrived below the wall one of the defenders pitched backward, thrust through the face by an Arsuuny spear. The Avtin was dead when she struck the ground with a clang of brass. Iroedh ran up the nearest steps to the top of the wall and looked over the parapet.

The Arsuuni had forehandedly brought along great carts full of scaling ladders, drawn by tame vakhnags, and they had rushed sixteens of these ladders against the wall. The Avtini had pushed some of them over backwards. Several Arsuuni who had fallen with the ladders lay writhing on the ground, for because of their size they could not stand so much of a fall as an Avtin.

On the ground outside, a giant in gold-plated armor walked up and down giving orders; this would be General Omvem of Tvaarm. Overhead the helicopter still whistled.

Now would be the time for Antis to appear with his drones, to take the Arsuuni in the rear. But there was no sign of him; not even a telltale cloud of dust on the road from Khinam.

"This way! This way!" cried voices on Iroedh's right, and the Avtini hurried toward the scene of the latest attack. A swarm of scaling ladders had been reared against the wall in that thinly held region, and up came the giants, shouting, *"Künnef! Künnef!"*

Iroedh made for one ladder that did not seem to have anybody watching it and started to push it away from the wall; then instinctively jerked back as a huge spearhead darted past her face. Before she could attack the ladder again the head and shoulders of an Arsuun appeared over the wall.

The long-jawed giant shifted her grip on her spear and braced herself for another stab at Iroedh. Iroedh rushed in, knocked the spearhead aside with her shield, and tried to hit the Arsuun in the face with the edge of the shield. The Arsuun brought up her own shield and for a second the shields ground together as each fighter tried to outmaneuver the other. Sensing the immense strength of her foe, Iroedh felt as if she were assailing a colossal bronze statue.

Then she caught a glimpse of the face as the shields separated, and thrust for the eyes with her machete. She felt the point go through tissue and bone, then jerked the blade out as the head of the giant pulled backward. Iroedh hacked again and again at the hateful face; then all at once there was no Arsuun there, and a great crash as the armored body struck the ground.

"Come, Queen!" shouted a worker. "Don't you hear the recall?"

Iroedh had been too busy with the Arsuuny soldier to heed the notes of the trumpet. Now she saw that everywhere the Avtini were leaping and tumbling down from the wall and running for the plaza in front of the main portal. The Arsuuni had already broken through the defense in one section and gained the wall, and the general was withdrawing her troops before they were cut up and destroyed piecemeal.

Iroedh ran down the steps with the rest, while behind her the Arsuuni swarmed over the wall with roars of *"Künnef!"*

The general, seeing Iroedh approach, cried: "I thought I told you not to fight! Don't you know that even queens have to obey me in warfare? Now get in the middle of the square. You can't accomplish anything with that overgrown fruit-knife, but we need you as a symbol."

"Oh, can't I?" protested Iroedh, waving her bloody blade, but the general caught her by the shoulders and pushed her into place. She was forming the Avtini into a massive hollow square, with spears and shields in double array around the outside to make a hedge that even the Arsuuni might have trouble piercing. A stream of workers rushed out of the domes with furniture and utensils which they piled in a crude barricade around the square.

"We still outnumber them," Iroedh heard the general say. Iroedh, however, knew that one Arsuun was worth two Avtini on a simple basis of size.

Iroedh looked over the ranks of the workers, between the helmeted heads. General Omvem of Tvaarm arrived in leisurely fashion and marshaled her soldiers for the final attack. It took the form of a wedge.

The deep Arsuuny trumpet groaned. The wedge thundered forward and struck the square with a deafening crash of clashing shields and snapping spears. Iroedh saw the point soldier of the wedge trip in climbing the barricade and fall, pierced by a dozen spears, and in her fall bowl over two Avtini. But those behind her pushed ahead, stabbing and trampling. The square gradually lost its shape and became a mere mass wrapped around the blunted point of the wedge. Those behind the front ranks tried to reach over the tangle of dead, wounded, and interlocked spear-shafts to get at their opponents.

The superior size of the Arsuuni told; beside Iroedh an Arsuuny spear-point struck down the general. Iroedh herself was buffeted by the crowd this way and that; elbows jabbed her in the face and heels stamped on her toes. An Arsuun towered over her, swinging a broken spear-shaft

150

as a club. Iroedh caught a blow on her shield and felt as if her arm had been broken.

Then the pressure eased and the noise became even louder. When Iroedh could see around her again, a swarm of armored drones was rushing down from the wall to form a phalanx advancing upon the Arsuuni from the rear. Before she could get her breath the drones struck the Arsuuni. Their front rank was armed entirely with machetes; these rushed in under the spears and slashed at the giants' legs where a hand's breadth of thigh showed between kilt and greave. Crash! Crash! Crash! Down went the Arsuuni like felled trees. Down went General Omvem, assailed by four drones at once.

The leaderless and surrounded Arsuuni milled around, trying to fight their way out, but the instant one separated from her fellows she was thrust through the legs from behind and fell. Crash! Crash!

And then there were no more giants on their feet: only a couple of hundred lying about the plaza, while the Avtini went around cutting the throats of those that still moved.

Iroedh was cutting one such throat when a pair of bloody hands hauled her to her feet. Antis hoisted her into the air, hugged the breath out of her, then gave her a stinging slap on the behind. From him it felt good.

"I told you not to get so far ahead!" he said. "We ran our legs off trying to catch up with you, and as it was we nearly arrived too late. We had three pieces of good luck to thank Gwyyr for. First we came across another rogue drone band who joined us. Second when we got to the Lhanwaed Hills we found that old Umwys had been forging matselhi ever since we left him; he had nearly a hundred. I bought the lot, and so armed more of my people with them than I had dared hope. Lastly the Arsuuni kindly left their ladders against the walls, so we came right up and over them. How have you made out?"

Iroedh found that, counting the defeats before the main battle, less than half the workers of Elham survived. Rhodh, for instance, had died fighting furiously; so had Tydh and Iinoedh and many of her other acquaintants. Only two officers, the royal officer and the grounds officer, lived. While the drones' losses had been negligible, the Arsuuni had been wiped out to the last giantess.

Iroedh told Antis what had happened, adding: "Now that Estir and the more conservative officers are gone, I hope they'll adopt our program for mating them with the drones."

151

"They'd better! After being filled to the ears with talk on the glories of married life, every rogue is mad with impatience to seize a worker and start stoking her with steak. And speaking of which . . ."

Antis gave her a piercing look whose meaning she had come to know well. However, the helicopter landed, to the intense curiosity of the Avtini who had not yet seen it, and Bloch got out.

"Congratulations on your victory!" he said.

"No thanks to you," said Antis sourly.

Iroedh said: "You forgot this, Antis." She swung her machete.

Bloch exclaimed: "You mean you never had anything like that before we came? And you copied it from us?"

"Yes."

"Oh, lord, now I'm in trouble! Didn't you tell me——"

"Yes, I fear I stretched the truth, but to save my people. We'll say nothing to the other Terrans and perhaps they will never know."

Bloch shook his head. "Let's hope they won't. I should have remembered what the swords of the Spanish conquistadores did to the poor Amerinds . . . But you wouldn't know about that. May I take some pictures, and remove a couple of dead Arsuuni? They'll be invaluable as specimens."

"Go right ahead," said Iroedh, shedding her bloody accouterments. "Oh, there's Vardh!"

Vardh was having a wounded arm tied up. The royal officer said to Iroedh:

"The others won't let Vardh live among them even if they adopt your scheme. Their horror of harming a queen is too great."

Vardh looked up. "I heard you. Since Iroedh now has Antis she doesn't need me any more, so I'll make things easy for all . . ."

She picked up a spear, held it horizontally in front of her so that the point touched her chest, and started to run toward the portal.

"Stop her!" cried Iroedh.

Antis, after one puzzled look, sprang after Vardh, caught her by the crest, and wrenched the spear away from her.

"Little fool!" he growled. "As if your Community hadn't lost enough of its people!"

Iroedh said: "There's no need to take your life, Vardh dear. I have a better program for you."

"What? To become a bulgy functional female like you

152

and submit to the horrid embraces of some drooling drone? No thank you!"

"How would you like to be the new Oracle of Ledhwid?"

"Me, an Oracle?"

"Yes. As the old one died without appointing a successor, the post is practically open to the first comer. I think it would suit you."

"I'll think it over," said Vardh. "Excuse my discourtesy, darling. I still love you, but everything's so confused."

Tregaros said: "Queen Iroedh, you should organize an immediate attack on Tvaarm. They'll have but a handful of soldiers and won't expect it, and their Avtiny slaves won't help them. A quick march and a night attack, eh? We can use their own ladders . . ."

The fellow was probably right, thought Iroedh, but she had seen about all the bloodshed she could stand for one day. She did not want Antis mixed up in such a project, because with his foolhardy bravery he would probably get himself killed. She said to the royal officer:

"Do the surviving members of the Council accept my program now?"

"Queen, we're so bewildered we don't know what to say. Let me speak to the grounds officer."

Presently the two officers came back to Iroedh. The royal officer said: "Queen Iroedh, we accept you and agree to legalize your mixed-diet program if you promise not to take away any of our constitutional liberties. Does that suit you?"

"Certainly."

The officer went off to organize burial squads, as there were far too many corpses for the soapworks to use. The surviving workers went about their task somberly, having, despite their spectacular victory, lost too many friends to cheer. While the dead were being disposed of Bloch said:

"Hey, Iroedh! Antis! I forgot to tell you that Subbarau has a position available for you."

"What?" said Antis.

"He can't transport you to Terra, but he can appoint you representatives of the *Viagens Interplanetarias* for the planet Ormazd. We always try to obtain a reliable native as an intermediary. To begin, you would accompany us on our tour of the other continents to familiarize yourselves with their cultures and languages."

"It sounds fascinating," said Iroedh, "but I must consult

Antis." When she got him aside she said: "What do you think? I'm all for it."

Antis looked dubious. "We have a good prospect here as king and queen of a new united bisexual Community, don't you think? What do you want to go flying off to the ends of nowhere for?"

"And what's a king or queen under the new dispensation? They used to need a queen to lay eggs, but if all workers become functional females, what use is a queen? We should have no political power, especially as they've warned me against tampering with their constitution."

"I don't know . . ." said Antis.

Iroedh said gently: "Are you afraid of the sky ship?"

"Me?" His expression changed at once. "I should say not! So if we stayed here we should be mere ornaments, deferred to but not allowed to *do* anything?"

"Exactly. While if we accept the Terran offer——"

"We shall never have a dull moment. As I've said all along, our destiny lies with the Terrans. Let's tell Daktablak quickly, before he changes his mind."

The royal officer was at Iroedh's elbow again. "Tregaros wants to organize a joint expedition to Tvaarm, and if you have no objections we'll set forth tomorrow. We have agreed, however, that you and Antis must stay here; we can't have you exposing yourselves in combat again."

"Suit yourselves," said Iroedh. "The sky folk have offered us a much bigger job than reigning over one Community."

"What's this?"

Iroedh told the officer about the Terran offer. Antis added: "She's quite right; after spending most of my life cooped up in the dronery, not even a continent is big enough for me."

"Great Eunmar!" said the royal officer. "This is a surprise. I hope we may continue to call you 'Queen' as an honorary title."

"Certainly. I'll even wear the regalia when I visit you, but you must have a set made for Antis too."

"We will. We need things to appeal to our sentiments, to keep us loyal to each other and to the Community——"

"Sentiment!" cried Iroedh. "That reminds me! I never did learn what happened to Elnora."

"Who or what is Elnora?" asked the royal officer.

"A character in a book which Daktablak's mate gave me. If I don't take another thing from Elham I want that book. But I wonder what became of it after I was driven out."

154

Vardh spoke up: "I took it from your cell and hid it in my own, thinking you might return someday for it. You'll find it under my pallet."

"Thank you, darling! I shall be right back."

She dashed into the portal. Antis said: "Wait, beautiful! I'm coming too!" and ran after her.

Glossary of Ormazdian Names and Words

Aithles—the king in the *Lay of Idhios.*
Antis—a drone of Elham and a close friend of Iroedh.
Arsuuni—a race hostile to the Avtini (in their own language, *Arshuul*).
Arsuunyk—the language of the Arsuuni.
Avpandh—a worker of Elham.
Avtini—the most civilized race of Ormazd (sing. *Avtin*).
Avtinid—the land of the Avtini.
Avtiny—adj., pertaining to the Avtini.
Avtinyk—the language of the Avtini.

Baorthus—a drone of Elham.
borb—a unit of distance comparable to a mile.
branio—"stop" in Avtinyk.

dairtel—a plant bearing a kind of nut.
Danoakor—an ancient reforming queen of the Avtini.
Denüp—a community of the Arsuuni.
Dhiis—a god of the ancient Avtiny religion.
dhug—a small spiny animal.
dhwyg—a many-legged creeping organism.
Dyos—a drone of Elham.

Eiudh—a worker of Elham.
Elham—the heroine's community of Avtini.
Elhamni—the inhabitants of Elham.
Enroys—a former Oracle of Ledhwid.
Estir—Crown Princess of Elham.

155

Eunmar—a goddess of the ancient Avtiny religion.
Garnedh—a priestess of Ledhwid.
Geyliad—a locale in the *Song of Geyliad*.
Gliid—an uninhabited valley near Thidhem.
Gogledh—a worker of Thidhem.
Gruvadh—a worker of Elham.
Gunes—a drone in the *Lay of Idhios*.
Gwyyr—the ancient Avtiny goddess of luck.

Hawardem—a northern Avtiny community.
Ho-olhed—the star Procyon.
hudig—a small edible hervibore.
huusg—a jellyfish-like marine organism (also a constellation).
Hwead—a gorge near Ledhwid.

Idhios—hero of the *Lay of Idhios*.
Igog—a fire-breathing monster in the *Tale of Mantes*.
Iinoedh—a worker of Elham.
Inimdhad—a place mentioned in the *Lay of Idhios*.
Intar—Queen of Elham.
Iroedh—a worker of Elham, and the heroine.
Ithodh—a worker of Yeym.

khal—a tree with edible seeds.
Khinad Point—a place near Elham.
Khinam—a ruined city on Khinad Point.
Khwiem—an Avtiny community.
künnef—the war cry of the Arsuuni.
Kutanas—a drone of Elham.
kwa—"Hurrah!" in Avtinyk.

Ledhwid—site of a famous oracle.
leipag—a medium-sized edible herbivore.
Lhanwaed—a range of hills near Elham.
Lhuidh—a priestess of Ledhwid.

Maiur—Queen of Thidhem.
Mantes—hero of the *Tale of Mantes*.
matselh—Avtinyk for "machete."

neiriog—a small animal tamed as a pet.
Niond—Avtinyk for "earth," "soil," or "world."
noag—a large carnivore.

oedhurh—Avtinyk for "love."
Omvem—general of Tvaarm.

Omvyr—Queen of Tvaarm (in her own language, *Om-förs*).

pandre-eg—a large wild herbivore related to the ueg.
Pligayr—Intar's predecessor as Queen of Elham.
pomuial—a flowering plant.
prutha—an exclamation of annoyance.

Rhodh—a worker of Elham.
Rhuar—a former queen of Elham.
rumdrekh—a system of self-defense.

Santius—a drone in the *Lay of Idhios*.
suroel—a plant whose fibers are used for textiles.
Sveik—Arsuunyk for "earth."

tarhail—a domesticated cereal grass.
telh—a flute.
Thidhem—a neighboring Avtiny community.
Tiwinos—a god of the ancient Avtiny religion.
Tregaros—a drone, an officer of Wythias.
Tvaarm—an Arsuuny community (in their own language, *Tvaar*).
Tydh—a worker of Elham.

ueg—a large bipedal domesticated draft animal.
uintakh—a game similar to tenpins.
umdhag—a small animal.
Umwys—a rogue drone, a smith.

vakhnag—a very large quadruped herbivore.
vakhwil—a tree whose bark is used for writing material.
valh—Avtinyk for "knife."
Vardh—a worker of Elham, a close friend of Iroedh.
Vinir—the queen in the *Lay of Idhios*.
vremoel—a fruit.

weu—an exclamation of sorrow.
Wisgad—a volcano near Gliid.
Wythias—leader of a band of rogue drones.

Yaedh—a priestess of Ledhwid.
Yeym—an Avtiny community destroyed by the Arsuuni.
Ystalverdh—a priestess of Ledhwid.
Ythidh—a worker of Elham.

Signet Science Fiction by Robert Silverberg

☐ **THE BOOK OF SKULLS.** From out of the past came a book offering immortality to those who would seek it, and four college students read the words which sent them on the strange quest that might end in immortality for two but must end in death for the others.

(#Q5177—95¢)

☐ **A TIME OF CHANGES.** The planet's fate lay in the hands of Prince Kinnal Darival, and within the prince's reach lay a drug which promised any man a meeting with Infinity, a drug which could spread throughout the planet and destroy it . . .   (#Q4729—95¢)

☐ **THOSE WHO WATCH.** A strange and seductive novel of three inadvertent colonists from outer space whose accidental encounter with Earth triggers interplanetary conflict. It is also the most unusual love story ever written.   (#T4496—75¢)

☐ **DOWNWARD TO THE EARTH.** Earthman Edmund Gundersen gambles his body and soul in an alien game where the stakes are immortality.   (#T4497—75¢)

THE NEW AMERICAN LIBRARY, INC.,
P.O. Box 999, Bergenfield, New Jersey 07621

Please send me the SIGNET BOOKS I have checked above. I am enclosing $_____(check or money order—no currency or C.O.D.'s). Please include the list price plus 15¢ a copy to cover handling and mailing costs. (Prices and numbers are subject to change without notice.)

Name_____

Address_____

City_____State_____Zip Code_____
Allow at least 3 weeks for delivery

More SIGNET Science Fiction You Will Enjoy

☐ **STARSWARM by Brian Aldiss.** Exciting science-fiction about a bizarre sub-human species struggling to survive on myriads of far-flung worlds.   (#T4558—75¢)

☐ **THE DARK SIDE OF THE EARTH by Alfred Bester.** Seven startling science-fiction tales by a prize-winning author.
(#T4402—75¢)

☐ **THE SHORES OF ANOTHER SEA by Chad Oliver.** Royce Crawford's African baboonery becomes a laboratory for a terrifying extraterrestrial experiment. From the author of the prize-winning novel **The Wolf Is My Brother.** "A prime contender for the Heinlein-Clarke front rank of genuine science-fiction."—The New York Times
(#T4526—75¢)

☐ **BY FURIES POSSESSED by Ted White.** A frightening adventure into the unknown where a manned satellite returns from a thirty year voyage into space.
(#T4275—75¢)

☐ **A CIRCUS OF HELLS by Poul Anderson.** The story of a lost treasure guarded by curious monsters, of captivity in a wilderness, of a journey through reefs and shoals that could wreck a ship, and of the rivalry of empires.
(#T4250—75¢)

SIGNET Science Fiction Titles by Robert A. Heinlein

☐ **THE MENACE FROM EARTH.** Title story plus The Year of the Jackpot, By His Bootstraps, Columbus Was a Dope, Sky Lift, Goldfish Bowl, Project Nightmare and Water Is for Washing. (#T4306—75¢)

☐ **THE DAY AFTER TOMORROW.** Six men set out to save America from annihilation armed only with two weapons: a controlled form of atomic energy and their own determination to defend their country against a deadly invasion. (#T4227—75¢)

☐ **METHUSELAH'S CHILDREN.** The year is 2125 and the Families, possessing extraordinary longevity, are forced to flee Earth on an untested starship. To their horror they discover the alien stars pose a threat even more terrifying than the one they fled. (#T4226—75¢)

☐ **THE PUPPET MASTERS.** The dean of science fiction describes America in the grip of invaders from another planet. "By any standard, this is first-rate entertainment, with likable characters, excitement and plenty of hard-boiled humor."—The New York Times (#T3752—75¢)

☐ **THE DOOR INTO SUMMER by Robert A. Heinlein.** An inventor of robots takes the "Deep Sleep"—suspended animation for thirty years—and wakes up, still a young man, in the bewildering 21st century. (#T3750—75¢)